Ken Ludwig's
Midsummer/Jersey

A Samuel French Acting Edition

SAMUELFRENCH.COM

ISBN 978-0-573-70076-7   Printed in U.S.A.   #20305

MUSIC USE NOTE

Licensees are solely responsible for obtaining formal written permission from copyright owners to use copyrighted music in the performance of this play and are strongly cautioned to do so. If no such permission is obtained by the licensee, then the licensee must use only original music that the licensee owns and controls. Licensees are solely responsible and liable for all music clearances and shall indemnify the copyright owners of the play and their licensing agent, Samuel French, Inc., against any costs, expenses, losses and liabilities arising from the use of music by licensees.

IMPORTANT BILLING AND CREDIT
REQUIREMENTS

All producers of *KEN LUDWIG'S MIDSUMMER/JERSEY must* give credit to the Author of the Play in all programs distributed in connection with performances of the Play, and in all instances in which the title of the Play appears for the purposes of advertising, publicizing or otherwise exploiting the Play and/or a production. The name of the Author must appear in conjunction with the title of the play on a separate line on which no other name appears, immediately above the title and must appear in size of not less than seventy-five percent of the size of the title type.

KEN LUDWIG'S *MIDSUMMER/JERSEY* premiered on November 17th, 2011 at James W. Robinson Jr. Secondary School. The production was directed by Douglas Rome, with assistant direction by Lizzie Hodgdon, dramaturgy by Sarah Irving*, set design by Emily Rowson*, set decoration by Hannah Sikora*, costumes by Arianna Vessal, sound design by Christine Wagner, lighting design by Paul Mayo*, property design by Mary Turgeon*, hair & makeup design by Kayla Neal, technical direction by Samantha Hennerty, set construction by Matt Lynch, paint by Lindsey Rubin, publicity by Sarah Irving*, program by Emily Rowson*, and film & video by Sean Cooper. It was stage managed by Allison Poms*, and assistant stage managed by Anna Barr*, Kyle Ronyecs and Helai Karim. The production was managed by Michaela Wright*. The cast was as follows:

MIA "COOKIE" DICARLO	Gabby Rojtman
HELENE	Emily Rowson*
LYLE "THE UNDERSTATEMENT" FAGIOLI	Ethan Malamud
DENIS	Kolya Rabinowitch
ROBIN GOODFELLOW (PUCK)	Adam Bradley*
OBERON	Dan Barr*
TITANIA	Sarah Irving*
NIKKI BOTTOM	Carys Meyer*
PATTI QUINCE	Molly Johnson*
CHRIS ATHENS	TJ Albertson*
HIPPOLYTA GINSBERG	Aubrey Benham*
PHYLLIS TRAIT	Hillary Hollaway
JUSTINE DICARLO	Hannah Sikora*
RUFUS DICARLO	Jackson Viccora*
PRINCIPAL PLATT	Addy Gravatte
FRANCI FLUTE	Sarah Marksteiner
TERRI THUMBS	Mary Turgeon*
ROBERT SUDDS	Jamie Green*
JANET SNUG	Brandy Skaddan
COBWEB	Taylor Fountain
MOONBEAM	Andie Matten
MOTH	Maya Davis*
MUSTARDSEED	Kate Poms
PEASEBLOSSOM	Ellie Duhadway
SUNFLOWER	Darla Reynolds
SUNSHINE	Kelly Thomas
TURTLE	Rachel Ingle

JACK . . . . Josh Meyers*

SHIRLEY . . . . Hannah Bunting*

KIM . . . . Meg Connors

MINDY . . . . Taryn Falkenstein

PENNY . . . . Jessica Israel

HAROLD . . . . Jacob Medley

BAKARI . . . . Ashaya Pokhrel

OBERON'S FAIRIES . . . .   Alex Bulova, Ashaya Pokhrel, Ivonte Milligan, Jacob Medley, James Lynch

TITANIA'S FAIRIES . . . . Taryn Falkenstein, Hannah Bunting

UNDERSTUDIES
Aubrey Benham*, Alex Bulova, Meg Connors, Maya Davis*, Monica Goodwin, Sydney Lykins, Andie Matten, Jacob Medley, Dasha Savina, Sophia Sempeles, Brionna Simmons, Arianna Vessal*

PRODUCTION TEAM
Amani Abdeljabbar, Sean Baird, Dan Bonilla, Hannah Bunting, Jorge Candia, Tristan Cheramie, Renee Colligan, Marissa Considine, Sean Cooper, Nicole Copenhaver, Liam Dillon, Sabina Dua, Casey Early, Emily Filostrat, Victoria Fong, Paige Franklin, Chloe Gilfoil, Monica Goodwin, Jamie Green, Blair Gruendl, Kyle Gaulke, Kelly Guin, Paige Hastie, Hillary Holloway, Molly Johnson, Brennan Laskas, James Lynch, Lucia Maldondo, Andie Matten, Chris Mayhew, Kayse McGough, Ivonte Milligan, Chris Moalli, Dinma Onyekwere, Kate Poms, Anna Ready, Kelsey Rooney, Lindsey Rubin, D'Arcy Sampson, Dasha Savina, Hannah Selz, Elana Shuart, Brandy Skaddan, Andrew Suarez, Isabella Suarez, Elise Truong, Reetu Varadhan, Sophie White, Cassie Wood, Edyan Yusuf

*Denotes Membership in International Thespian Society

KEN LUDWIG'S *MIDSUMMER/JERSEY* was subsequently presented by Interlochen Center for the Arts (William Church, Director of Theatre and Comparative Arts) on July 27, 2012. The production was directed by J. W. Morrissette, with assistant direction by Linda Osborn, dramaturgy by Scott Harman, set design by Christopher Dills, costumes by Candace Hughes, sound design by Bryan Chess, and lighting design by Jason Banks. It was stage managed by Seth Valentine. The cast was as follows:

PRINCIPAL PLATT/MOTE	Lily Lipman
GOVERNOR CHRIS ATHENS	Will Ouweleen
HIPPOLYTA GINSBERG	Tara Stallion
PHYLLIS TRAIT/COBWEB	Margaret Murphy
JUSTINE DICARLO	Natasha Batten
RUFUS DICARLO/JACK/TURTLE	Clayton To
MIA "COOKIE" DICARLO	Cate Payne
LYLE "THE UNDERSTATEMENT" FAGIOLI	Harry Thornton
DENIS	Abram Blau
HELENE	Sarah Pidgeon
OBERON	Andrew Elk
TITANIA	Chloe Baldwin
ROBIN GOODFELLOW (PUCK)	Jennifer Klink
PATTI QUINCE	Shawna James
NIKKI BOTTOM/HAROLD	Amrita Newton
FRANCI FLUTE/BAKARI	Ruby Green
JANET SNUG/PENNY	Maddy Sosnowski
ROBERTA SUDDS/SHIRLEY	Savannah Kolodziej
TERRI THUMBS/MINDY	Emma Gutt
PEASBLOSSOM	Hannah Dalessio
MOONBEAM	Paige Goetz
SUNFLOWER	Clare Donaldson
SUNSHINE	Grace DiChristina
MUSTARDSEED	Carolyn Rogan
TURTLE	Clayton To

Understudies

MIA	Lily Lipman
OBERON	Will Ouweleen
TITANIA	Margaret Murphy
HELENE	Natasha Batten
LYLE	Clayton To
PUCK	Ruby Green

FOREWORD

A Midsummer Night's Dream is one of the two or three greatest stage comedies in the English language. Yet there are parts of the play – as there are parts of all of Shakespeare's plays – that can be confusing to a modern audience. Not surprisingly, the vocabulary and syntax of the Elizabethan era were somewhat different than they are today, and Shakespeare as written, especially without some form of assistance, can sometimes feel like a foreign language. With this in mind, I wrote *Midsummer/Jersey*, at least in part, to make *A Midsummer Night's Dream* more accessible to modern audiences.

My strategy has been a simple one: I've tried to retell the story of *A Midsummer Night's Dream* in a contemporary setting using characters who are not only modern in type (in this case the denizens of New Jersey beach society), but of a kind who shed fresh light on their Shakespearean models. When we get past the difficulties of Elizabethan language, Hermia, Helena, Lysander and Demetrius are the zippiest of teenagers, full of heart and hope, mischief and hormonal longing. Their counterparts in *Midsummer/Jersey* – Mia, Helene, Lyle and Denis – are meant to remind us that Shakespeare's characters are virtually identical to the teenagers we meet today.

As for the play as a whole, I've tracked the original act-by-act, scene-by-scene and often speech-by-speech, in the hope that enjoyment of the modern play will take readers back to the original armed with a kind of structural road map. It is easy for students to look on Shakespeare as an uphill battle, and there are plenty of adults who share the view of the great comic playwright George S. Kaufman that Shakespeare is about a lot of kings who never get to sit down. The truth, of course, is vastly different; and it is one of the goals of *Midsummer/Jersey* to send as many people as possible back to *A Midsummer Night's Dream* with tools for understanding its miraculous architecture. The structure of the play is simply breathtaking: In five acts it juggles four separate comic plots, and there isn't a minute of confusion or boredom from start to finish. If the play were a building, it would be Buckingham Palace and the Taj Mahal rolled into one.

Part of my love for *A Midsummer Night's Dream* is Shakespeare's remarkable idea of pitting the fairy world against the down-to-earth world of the lovers and the tradesmen. The idea is so simple and ingenious that the notion of updating the setting to almost any society with well-defined social classes – including the New Jersey beach culture – became increasingly obvious the more I worked on the play. But updating implies currency, and it is important to the success of *Midsummer/Jersey* that the cultural references in the play continue to feel modern to every new audience. For this reason, I hope that future directors of *Midsummer/Jersey* will make an effort to keep the play's cultural references as up-to-date as possible. The musical choices, for example, should (with copyright permission) be taken from the playlists of the hottest radio stations in town, and the references to clothing, hair styles, slang and gadgets should come straight out of the latest issues of *Seventeen*, *Vanity Fair*, *People* and *Cosmopolitan*. During the initial production of the play, for example, I was reminded by one of the actors that my hair salon needed a tanning bed. It was an actor's idea to have Roberta played by a stylish male hairdresser named Robert. And the ending of the first act felt a little flat until someone suggested a 20-second tag where the entire cast danced to a chorus of *The Party Rock Anthem* (*"Every day I'm shufflin'…"*).

When all is said and done, my hopes for *Midsummer/ Jersey* are simple but profound: that this play can be added to the hundreds of other tributes in our culture to what many people consider the greatest comedy ever written.

Ken Ludwig
February 2012

CHARACTERS

PRINCIPAL PLATT
GOVERNOR CHRIS ATHENS
HIPPOLYTA - his fiancé
PHYLLIS TRAIT - his secretary
JUSTINE DICARLO - his chief of staff
RUFUS DICARLO - her husband
MIA "COOKIE" DICARLO
LYLE "THE UNDERSTATEMENT" FAGIOLI
DENIS - in love with Mia
HELENE - in love with Denis
PATTI QUINCE
NIKKI BOTTOM
FRANCI FLUTE
TERRI THUMBS
ROBERTA SUDDS or **ROBERT SUDDS**
JANET SNUG
OBERON
TITANIA
ROBIN GOODFELLOW (Puck)
OBERON'S FAIRIES (optional)
Titania's Fairies:
> **MOONBEAM**
> **SUNFLOWER**
> **SUNSHINE**
> **TURTLE**
> **PEASEBLOSSOM**
> **MUSTARDSEED**
> **COBWEB**
> **MOTE**

CAST SIZE

Without doubling, 27 actors, 22 women and 5 men. In the original production, the director added a train of male fairies for Oberon, and this added 8 additional male actors to the cast. But all the fairies can be of either gender, and the cast size and composition is extremely flexible. Doubling can reduce the cast to 14.

In memory of
Peter Herzberg,
finest friend
and
New Jersey native.

This volume is also dedicated
to the kids at
Robinson High School
who premiered the play.

ACT ONE

Prologue

(A high school auditorium in Wildwood, New Jersey. There is a podium in the middle of the stage and **PATRICIA PLATT***, the principal of the school is standing behind it. She is an intelligent middle-aged woman with a nice sense of irony.)*

PRINCIPAL PLATT. Good afternoon, boys and girls.

(Kids are stationed in various parts of the auditorium and they answer "Good morning, Miss Platt!")

As Principal of Wildwood High School here in Wildwood, New Jersey, I want to welcome all of you to the last assembly of our school year.

(clap, clap)

Thank you for your enthusiasm. Now as you know, it is our tradition here at Wildwood to allow you to vote for your guest speakers for the final assembly, and I will confess that I was personally hoping you would invite the newly-appointed Director of the New Jersey Transport Commission, the exciting Doctor Irving Comglot. But no, no, it was your decision to invite two other alumni of this school who have made their names by appearing on a reality television series entitled *(checking her notes, bemused)* "Smokin' Hot in Jersey: The Loose and the Luscious." Now I'm sorry to report that while these two individuals did in fact graduate from here six short years ago, they did so with the two lowest grade-point averages in the history of the school. They were also suspended a total of thirteen times – so I'm afraid that our board of directors determined at their last meeting that these two individuals should *not* be invited to speak to you at our gathering today.

(groan)

However…on this occasion, I decided to *overrule* the board, because I know that you all worked very hard this year, and frankly, you deserve a break,

(The kids sit up straight and start listening)

and so, though I may end up regretting this decision, please welcome Mia DiCarlo and Lyle Fagioli, known throughout the country as Cookie and the Understatement.

(Very hip music starts blaring from the speakers and there is a roar from the audience. The kids go wild as **COOKIE** *(aka* **MIA**) *and* **THE UNDERSTATEMENT** *(aka* **LYLE**) *enter from the back of the theater and down the aisle. To judge by appearances, they are the* ne plus ultra, *the height of coolness, the bomb itself.)*

LYLE. Heya guys.

MIA. Yo, high school.

LYLE. Hey keep it cool, will ya? I'm goin' deaf up here.

(The crowd laughs and quiets down.)

MIA. So, anyway, like it's cool to be back, you know. Next to my Guido here.

LYLE. Yeah, that's me.

MIA. I mean, we don't have a lot to say up here, but then I never even got to assembly when I was a kid, I was in the Principal's office most of the day.

LYLE. Me too, though I am in fact quite a good pubic speaker.

MIA. That's *public* speaker, you idiot.

LYLE. Sorry.

Hey, don't criticize!

MIA. So the thing is, we've got like two announcements to make. Number one is, our television show, "Smokin'

Hot in Jersey: the Loose and the Luscious" has just been renewed for Season Six, startin' this Sunday at nine on the Mormon Channel.

(Kids: "Yeeahhhh!")

LYLE. And the other thing is, we've decided to come out in the open about somethin', which is … that Mia and I have been… well, we've been married since we left high school. About six years now.

*(Hubbub: "No way!" "I don't believe it!" "They're married?" "Go, Cookie!" – and now some of the kids (**JACK**, **LILI**, **CHELSEA**, **BAKARI**, **KIM**, and **OLIVIA**) stand up and start asking questions:)*

JACK. But Lyle, you're the Understatement! How could you do it?!

LYLE. You know how it is, man. Young and stupid.

*(**MIA** gives him a dope slap.)*

Hey, I'm jokin', I'm jokin'!

LILI. Was it like a bun in the oven?

MIA. Are you kiddin' me?!

LYLE. Hey, come on, I respect this girl. She was my girl-friend!

CHELSEA. So how did it happen?

BAKARI. How'dja get married?

KIM. Who asked who?

MIA. Shall we tell 'em?

LYLE. They won't believe it.

MIA. Let's tell 'em anyway. We've got like a half hour left and I don't have nothin' else to say.

LYLE. You wanna start?

MIA. You go ahead.

LYLE. Okay. So. Everybody, I want you to close your eyes and imagine yourselves, six years ago – we were just outa high school – and we are at a rally for the Governor of New Jersey.

OLIVIA. The Governor Governor?

JACK. You mean Governor Athens?

MIA. Yeah, that's him. My mom works for him. She's his Chief of Staff. We were at this really cool election rally with posters and little flags and stuff, and it was about this time that the Governor was planning to get married himself.

(The set starts changing.)

LYLE. So I want you to think of us lookin' six years younger, and imagine yourselves at this rally. He's standin' there with his fiancé, Hippolyta Ginsberg.

MIA. And she's standin' over here, lookin' up at him hopin' he'll get reelected. And he turns to her and he says

LYLE. Now fair Hippolyta, our wedding hour
Draws on apace.

MIA. The Governor talks like that. He's an intellectual.

LYLE. Four happy days bring in
Another moon; but O, methinks how slow
This old moon wanes. She lingers my desires
Like to a step dame or a dowager
Long withering out a young man's revenue.

Scene One

(And we're at the rally. **GOVERNOR ATHENS** *is in his early 40s, young and hip, a decent fellow, and* **HIPPOLYTA** *is the perfect wife for him. Smart, upbeat, and sensitive.)*

*(***ATHENS*** *joins the opening speech on about the 4th line.* **LYLE** *finishes the speech with him, then disappears along with* **MIA** *and the high school.)*

ATHENS. She lingers my desires
Like to a step dame or a dowager
Long withering out a young man's revenue.

HIPPOLYTA. *(side-stepping* **ATHENS**' *advance)*
Four days will quickly steep themselves in night,
Four nights will quickly dream away the time,
Which means you've got to cool it, baby, and wait
For the wedding. It's only four days away.

ATHENS. Thanks a lot, but it won't be easy. *(calling off)* Miss Trait?!

PHYLLIS. Yes, Governor?

*(***PHYLLIS TRAIT*** *enters. She's the Governor's secretary, and she carries a notepad.)*

ATHENS. How are the plans for the wedding coming along?

PHYLLIS. Oh, excellent, sir. Lots of pomp and merriment.

ATHENS. No problems, then?

PHYLLIS. No, sir. Well. There has been a suggestion by the arts community that some form of public entertainment be provided, and I thought why not? We'll let a number of amateur acting groups prepare a little something and then we'll choose the winner *that day*, at the wedding, among the rivals. And it's not as if they'll have wasted their time, I mean, how hard can it be, it's only theater.

MIA. *(off) GOVERNOR!*

JUSTINE. *(off) Mia, stop it! You may not bother the Governor, and* *that is the –*

MIA. *(off) Leave me alone!*

JUSTINE. *(off) Just stop it young lady!*

MIA. *(off) Don't touch me!*

JUSTINE. *(off) I am your mother!!*

MIA. *(off) And I'm your daughter and my life is at stake!*

> *(At which point, **MIA DICARLO** runs in. She's **COOKIE** at seventeen, played by the same actress. She's followed on by **LYLE** and another young man of the same age named **DENIS**. All three of them are Italian-Americans from New Jersey. For the boys this means that they're buff, self-confident, and use pomade. For the girls (and we'll soon meet another one) this means that they're cheeky, tan, and emotional. Like waterfowl, they migrate each summer to the Jersey shore for mating purposes.)*

> *(Racing in behind them is **JUSTINE DICARLO**, Mia's mother, who, as we know, is Governor Athens' Chief of Staff. She was once a Jersey shore girl herself but now, alas, she is that nemesis of all things spontaneous and joyful, an adult.)*

MIA. *Governor, I gotta talk to you!*

ATHENS. Mia?

MIA. Governor, I need you to give me one of those whatdy-acallits. Dispensations. Y'know like the Pope does only then it's holy.

ATHENS. I don't know what you –

JUSTINE. Governor, I am *so* sorry. Mia should *not* be disturbing you like this –

ATHENS. Mia, what's the trouble? Maybe I can –

MIA. I want to get married, okay?! To Lyle here.

LYLE. How ya doon? How ya doon?

MIA. But Ma is saying no *for no good reason!*

JUSTINE. You are seventeen years old! How is *that* for a reason?! You may not get married without my consent until you are eighteen years old and that is the law! *(to **ATHENS**)* She met him four weeks ago in a hot tub.

And now she wants to break up with *Denis,* who is like one of the family.

DENIS. Hey what's happenin'.

MIA. Ma, what do you want from me, I'm in love with Lyle.

JUSTINE. Oh, please.

MIA. Hey I'm Italian! I do things on impulse.

JUSTINE. Which should not include marrying a man you met under water!

JUSTINE. People buy groceries on impulse! Or books! But this is –

MIA. You know if you wanted an Irish girl you should have got one

MIA. *now would you please stop nagging!!*

JUSTINE. *Mia!! (to* **ATHENS,** *referring to* **LYLE***)* Do you hear that?! That is *his* influence.

LYLE. *(pleased)* D'ya think?

DENIS. She was *my girlfriend,* ya know. You stole her from me.

LYLE. Get outa here! She was tired of you and I wonder why.

DENIS. Do you wonder why?

LYLE. Yeah I wonder why.

(They shove each other.)

JUSTINE. *Boys, stop it!*

MIA. *Ma!*

JUSTINE. Everything was fine until this Lyle came along and started turning her head, bewitching her with *iTunes cards* and rings and bracelets made of his *greasy hair.*

MIA. *(showing off the bracelet to* **HIPPOLYTA***)* Pretty nice, huh.

HIPPOLYTA. Ooh I love it.

JUSTINE. I'll send you to boarding school in Switzerland, young lady! You can join the Von Trapp family and *go sing about GOATS ON A HILLSIDE!!!*

ATHENS. *(to* **MIA***)* What does your father say?

MIA. He's afraid to talk to her.

ATHENS. You do need your parents' consent until you're eighteen.

MIA. But that's eleven months away! *(She starts weeping.)* I mean you're killin' me here! You might as well send me to a convent or somethin'!

ATHENS. Mia, to you your mother should be as a god.

(Beat. Then the kids start hooting with laughter.)

And your mother obviously thinks a lot of Denis.

LYLE. Then *she* can marry him.

ATHENS. Was I speaking to you?!

LYLE. Hey Gov, I'm sorry, but I'm as good as he is, ya know. We're both in technical college. Our grades are the same. On top of which, he's been foolin' around with Helene, who's Mia's friend who works at the lobster place down in Matawan. And he took her to a *club* and now she *dotes* on the guy!

MIA. *(still in tears)* Governor, Lyle and I are deeply, deeply in love. Doesn't that count for *somethin' in this world?!*

ATHENS. I'm afraid it doesn't in this case, Mia. The law is the law. *(to* **HIPPOLYTA***)* Am I right?

HIPPOLYTA. *(clearly on* **MIA***'s side)* Don't touch me.

(She walks away.)

ATHENS. *(hard)* Denis. Justine. I'd like to speak to both of you if you don't mind. Now.

(He leaves, followed by **DENIS**, **JUSTINE** *and* **PHYLLIS**. *This leaves* **MIA** *and* **LYLE** *alone on stage.)*

MIA. Oh, Lyle, what are we gonna do?!

LYLE. "The course of true love never did run smooth."

MIA. Hey, that's good.

LYLE. It's not mine. It's from that play we did last year about Helen Keller. But we're not alone in all of this, ya know. I mean there's like hundreds of reasons that love does not always run smooth in this world. For example, say the parents of the guy don't like the girl he's in love with so they put a contract out on her.

That could spoil things. Or what if you died, like out of the blue from some horrible, painful disease, huh? That could mess things up for us as a couple. Ya see, life is full of changes, Mia. It moves as fast as lightning.

MIA. Yeah.

LYLE. "So quick bright things come to confusion."

MIA. Helen Keller?

LYLE. *Avatar.*

MIA. Wow.

LYLE. Now listen, I've got an idea. I have an aunt, my father's sister once removed, and I'm like a son to her. She lives in Montreal and from what I hear the laws are different up there and so your age won't be a problem. Apparently they speak French so they can't even *ask* us about it. So if you love me –

MIA. Oh I do, I do!

LYLE. you gotta sneak outa your house tomorrow night and meet me in the woods near the beach. You know where I mean, behind the changing hut with the wonky shower. I'll wait there for you.

MIA. Oh, Lyle. I swear to you by the plastic cupid
On that box of chocolates that you once bought me.

LYLE. Aw.

MIA. And by the lyrics of our favorite Beatles song,
Doctor Pepper.

LYLE. Sergeant Pepper.

MIA. Sergeant Pepper.

(They cross themselves.)

MIA. By all the lyrics that I ever spoke,

LYLE. By all the iPods that I ever broke,

MIA. By the day we met and started mergin',

LYLE. By the remix of Madonna's *Like A Virgin,*

MIA. By all the shows I've watched on MTV,

LYLE. Tomorrow truly will I meet with thee.

MIA. Look, here comes Helene!

(HELENE enters. She's a taller, lankier version of Mia, the kind of good-natured girl you'd like to have as your best friend so you could help her survive her tangled love-life.)

LYLE. Hey how ya doon'? You're lookin' juice.

HELENE. You say I'm lookin' juice but look at Mi.

If I looked like her of happiness I'd die.

Cause Denis thinks that she's so juice and tan,

He calls me the Prisoner of Azkaban.

To him I'm nothing and he should be mine.

Oh teach me how to make my juice and his combine!

Oh, Mia, how could you do this to me?!

MIA. Helene, it's not my fault! I keep tellin' him in the nicest possible way, with class, I say, "Denis, listen carefully. When I look at you I could vomit." But he keeps comin' at me like somethin' outa *The Exorcist* or somethin'. But hey, guess what? He's gonna be all yours in no time.

HELENE. What are you talkin'?

MIA. Lyle and I are gettin' outa here. We're goin' to France.

LYLE. Canada.

MIA. You said they speak French! Whatever. Anyway, we're gettin' married there.

HELENE. Get outa here!

MIA. On my mother's grave.

HELENE. Wow.

MIA. See, tomorrow night, Lyle and I are meeting at the changing hut with the wonky shower and then we're makin' a run for it. So you take good care of yourself, okay? It could be a while till we see each other.

HELENE. Best friends forever.

MIA. BFF.

HELENE. You know it.

(They embrace.)

MIA. And say a prayer for us, okay?

HELENE. I will.

MIA. And good luck with Denis. If he doesn't marry you, I'll come back and beat the crap out of him.

HELENE. You got it.

MIA. *Lyle.*

LYLE. Yo.

MIA. See you tomorrow.

LYLE. Yeah sure. Cause
"we must starve our sight
From lovers' food, till morrow, deep midnight."

MIA. *Avatar?*

LYLE. *The Simpsons.*

MIA. Whoa.

LYLE. Helene, be good.

(**MIA** *and* **LYLE** *kiss, then exit in opposite directions.*)

HELENE. *(alone)* How lucky can you get? Do you know there are Guidos in Jersey who would like jump off buildings for me. They think I'm prettier than she is, but so what? Denis doesn't think so. He just can't see what they see in me. You see, love doesn't look through the eyes, it looks through the mind. If you *think* something ought to be pretty, then it *is* pretty, through *your* eyes. It's like in the movie *King Kong* where that girl falls in love with the big ape? He has these jaws that could like bite through a Ford Mustang, but she thinks he's cute as a button and wants to marry him. Can you imagine what their kids would be like? *"Hey, honey, come look! The neighbors' baby is chewing on our Camaro!"*

When Denis and I were still going out together, he used to turn to me and say, "Hey listen, I got a question for you." And I'd say, "What?" And he'd say, "How come I love you so much." And I'd say, "Cut it out, ask something serious." And he'd say, "Okay, *why is it* that I love you so much." And I'd yell, "Stop it! Ask me somethin' real!" And he'd say, "Okay. *How could it be* that I love you so much." And I would like melt into his armpit. And then one day he saw Mia walking down the street, and I could see from the look on his face what *he* was seeing when he looked at *her*, and it broke my heart like a stale cracker. *(She gets an idea …)* But wait. Hold it. I'm getting something good.

I'll tell Denis about their meeting in the wood.

Then he'll go after *her*, she'll say, "No dice,"

Then he'll thank *me* for being extra nice,

Which then in turn is gonna change his mood

So that he falls in love with me again.

In gratitude!

Ha ha!

It's gonna work!!!

… Or maybe it's not and I'll be up the creek,

Seeking the love that all of us must seek.

Wish me luck.

(She hurries off.)

(end of scene)

Scene Two

(We're inside a hairdressing salon along the boardwalk in a modest area of Atlantic City just after closing time. We see the usual chairs with dryers attached, along with mirrors, curlers, and those endless stacks of gossip magazines on all the tables. We also see a sign that says:

HAIR AND GONE.

HAIR. NAILS. TANNING. MANICURES.

When the lights come up, the employees [all female but one] are tidying up at the end of the day. **PATTI QUINCE** *is showing someone out.* **PATTI** *is the owner of the shop, a beanstalk in her mid-40s with bright red lipstick and unruly hair.)*

PATTI. Thank you for coming, Mrs. Falcone. You look ten years younger. If the men start getting frisky around you, just hit 'em with your cane. Good-bye, dear!

(When the client is gone, **PATTI** *pulls down the shade and calls out to her staff.)*

PATTI. Are we all here?!

NIKKI. *I'm here!*

FRANCI. Here.

TERRI. Yo!

ROBERT. Present.

JANET. *(the shy one)* I…yes.

NIKKI. I think you should call them one at a time and tell them what parts they have.

PATTI. Yes, I know. *Thank* you. Now here is the cast list with the names of all the actresses in the play which we hope *to God* will be chosen for the Governors' wedding day!

(squeals of delight)

NIKKI Yesss! Now tell them the name of the play and what it's about.

PATTI. The play is called *Romeo and Juliet* and it is about true love and its dreadful consequences.

ALL. Oooh.

NIKKI. It's by William Shakespeare who's very hot at the moment.

PATTI. Now I will call your names out one by one and tell you what parts you're playing. All right? Nikki Bottom, Stylist.

NIKKI. Ready! Ohhh, what part do I have? I can't wait!

PATTI. Nikki, I want you to play Romeo.

(Oooh. Aaah.)

NIKKI. Oh, I love that part! I love it! That is exactly who I wanted to play! But just remind me, is he good or bad?

PATTI. He is very good. He's a sort of Italian playboy who kills himself for love.

NIKKI. Ooh I like that, it's so touching. I'll weep buckets when I play him and the audience will suffer right along with me. *"Oh my love! I must end it all!"* And yet my favorite types are usually very strong women, like Bella in *New Moon*.

"Jacob! Don't you touch Edward! He can't help it if his teeth are sharp! That's how God made him!"

(applause from the other girls)

Thank you, thank you. Does Romeo have any moments like that?

PATTI. Not exactly. Franci Flute, Tanning Specialist.

FRANCI. I'm here, Patti.

PATTI. Franci, I want you to play Juliet.

FRANCI. Is he a playboy, too?

PATTI. No, she's a girl. The beautiful girl that Romeo is in love with. She also kills herself, but only after a long speech.

NIKKI. Oh let me play Juliet, too! You see I can pop in and out, I'm here, I'm there, I'm Romeo, I'm Juliet, they won't even notice. And I can play Romeo with a beard and a very masculine voice, *"Oh Juliet, what light you shed in yonder breaking window!"*

PATTI. No, no, no! You will play Romeo and Franci will play Juliet!

NIKKI. All right, fine. Fine! Go on.

PATTI. Robert Sudds, Shampoo.

ROBERT. Right here, Patti.

PATTI. Robert, you'll play Juliet's mother.

ROBERT. You got it.

PATTI. Terri Thumbs, Massage.

TERRI. Yo.

PATTI. Terri, you'll play the Friar.

TERRI. The fryer?

PATTI. That's right.

TERRI. You mean like a chicken?

PATTI. No, that's a deep fryer. You play a religious friar, which is like a priest except you've got a robe and a tassel.

TERRI. *(touching her chest)* I wear a tassel?

PATTI. I'll explain later. And that leaves Janet Snug, Manicures.

JANET. I-I'm here, Patti.

(**JANET** *is extremely shy.*)

PATTI. Janet, you'll play the lion's part.

ROBERT. Are you sure there's a lion in *Romeo and Juliet?*

PATTI. Well there wasn't, but I added one. Shakespeare is all well and good, but he can get tedious if you don't goose him up a little.

JANET. I-I hope you have the part written down because I'm a little slow of study.

PATTI. Not a problem. You can improvise because it's nothing but roaring.

NIKKI. Oh let me play the lion, too! You see roaring is my specialty! I-I-I go to the zoo all the time and listen to those strapping beasts and just let 'er rip. *Rooooar! Rooooar!*

PATTI. And you'll scare everybody at the wedding and get us all arrested!

FRANCI. The Governor will have bodyguards, Nikki!

TERRI. And bodyguards have guns!

ROBERT. Guns?

JANET Guns?

TERRI. Okay, I'm outa here.

THE OTHERS. *(leaving)* Me, too. / Get outa the way. / I'll see you later. / Bye-bye, now.

PATTI. *Stop! (to* **NIKKI***)* You will play Romeo and nothing else! Case closed!

*(***NIKKI*** is offended and starts to leave.)*

Because Romeo is the *star*, Nikki. He's a gentleman, he has his own office, and he barely leaves the stage for a minute! And so we need you, darling. Do it for the theater!

NIKKI. … All right, I'll do it.

(general relief)

But I'll need a beard. A sort of Brad Pitt look with a little stubble…

PATTI. Ladies! Here are the scripts, I beg you to be let-ter-perfect by our first rehearsal, tomorrow night by moonlight near the beach behind the changing hut with the wonky shower. I'd have us rehearse here in town, but you can imagine all the *imitators* who would try to steal our best ideas. The theater, as you know, is lechery incarnate.

NIKKI. We will meet at the beach, as Patti says, and there we shall rehearse most obscenely and courageously. And remember: we are artists. Our business is beauty. And so be perfect and remember our motto:

ALL. Scissors up
Nails bright
Combs down
Curlers tight.

Dryers on
Extra fluff
Hit the spray
And that's the stuff.

(They cheer.)

(end of scene)

ACT TWO

Scene One

(Somewhere on a rocky beach near the woods. Evening.)

(It would be a perfectly ordinary setting if it did not contain a world of fairies of all kinds: elves, sprites, brownies, pixies and pucks. Since these fairies live near the beach, they wear hip, fashionable beachwear.)

(As the lights come up, MOONBEAM enters, all in a dither. She's carrying a tray with cups filled with flowers and bottles of dew and begins hurriedly setting them out for a party. As she dashes from table to table, ROBIN GOODFELLOW enters and watches her with amusement. ROBIN is a male puck but can be played by an actress as a trousers role.)

ROBIN. How now, spirit?

MOONBEAM. *Ah!*

ROBIN. Wither wander you?

MOONBEAM. Under sun, under moon,
Through ocean, through waves,
Over beach, over sand,
Through castle, through caves,
I do wander everywhere,
Over here –

SUNFLOWER. *(popping up somewhere else on stage)* And over there!

SUNSHINE. *(ditto)* But at the moment, we have a party to put on.

PEASEBLOSSOM. *(scurrying in, carrying a present with a bow that isn't finished yet) Aghhh! Look at the time!* Here, quick, finger.

(She's asking **ROBIN** *to put his finger on the knot so she can finish tying the bow.)*

MOONBEAM. You aren't finished yet?

PEASEBLOSSOM. Don't start with me. Who got up early this morning and talked the crickets into providing the music?

(They all listen and we hear noisy crickets.)

SUNFLOWER. You call that music?

PEASEBLOSSOM. *(scornful)* They're tuning up.

(She snaps her fingers and rock music begins to play, the latest number-one single at the time of production. Simultaneously the lights change, the party starts and a new wave of fairies arrive in party dress. Candles flicker on the tables, fairy lights appear in strings, and drinks start getting passed around. Perhaps a mirrored ball descends from nowhere and starts spinning. Soon everyone is dancing.)

ROBIN. You're having a party?

SUNSHINE. The boy is quick.

ROBIN. But who's it for?

SUNFLOWER. The Queen.

ROBIN. The Queen?!

MOONBEAM. And *of* the Queen and *by* the Queen,

ALL THE FAIRIES. She shall not perish from the earth.

ROBIN. The Queen of the Fairies?!

SUNFLOWER. It's not the Queen of England, Sunshine.

ROBIN. I thought *you* were Sunshine.

SUNFLOWER. Sunflower.

SUNSHINE. Sunshine!

MOONBEAM. Moonbeam.

MOTE. Mote.

COBWEB. Cobweb.

TURTLE. Turtle.

ROBIN. Turtle?

TURTLE. I'm of mixed race.

ROBIN. Houston, we have a problem.

MUSTARDSEED. What's the matter?

ROBIN. The King doth keep *his* revels here tonight.

Take heed the Queen comes not within his sight.

They're having an argument.

TURTLE. Oh they argue all the time.

MOTE. At the drop of a hat.

COBWEB.   Or a wing.

PEASEBLOSSOM.   Or any old thing.

SUNSHINE. What's it about?

ROBIN. Don't you keep up with the palace intrigues? *(He pulls out a copy of* People Magazine *and starts pointing things out in one of the articles.)* Look. She forgot his birthday, and he wanted a Mustang.

SUNSHINE. The horse?

ROBIN. The car. He has the best muscle car collection in Fairy Land. He says it makes him feel young again.

(At this moment, **MIA** *and* **LYLE** *dash in, hand in hand. They stop suddenly and look back, hoping they haven't been followed.)*

MIA. *(to* **SUNSHINE**) Excuse me. Have you seen an annoying old woman who's trying to suffocate her daughter by being too strict about *everything?*

SUNSHINE. My mother's here?

*(***LYLE** *and* **MIA** *rush off. A moment later,* **DENIS** *dashes in and looks around.)*

DENIS. *(to* **TURTLE**) Hi, I'm Denis. I'm lookin' for a girl named Mia, about so high with a red scarf and a shoulder bag.

TURTLE. She went that way.

DENIS. Thanks!

(He kisses **TURTLE** *on the cheek and runs off.)*

TURTLE. *(touching her cheek)* That was the best relationship I've had in months.

(At which point **HELENE** *dashes on. She stops and looks around desperately in every direction.)*

ROBIN. *(pointing in the wrong direction on purpose)* Thataway.

HELENE. Thanks!

(She dashes off.)

ROBIN. Hahahahahahahahahaha!

MOONBEAM. Either I mistake your shape and attitude
    Or else you are that shrewd and knavish dude
    Called Robin Goodfellow.

SUNFLOWER. And they call you Puck, right?

ROBIN. Knock knock.

MOONBEAM. Who's there?

ROBIN. Puck.

MOONBEAM. Puck who?

ROBIN. Puck you! Hahahahahaha!

COBWEB. Sometimes like lobster he escapes the sea
    And clambers on the dock and wanders free
    And frightens all the girls until they bray
    And hold their swimsuits as they run away!

ROBIN. *That's me! That's me!*
    I jest to Oberon and make him smile
    When at the parties on the beach I rile
    The couples when they're dancing close like this.
    I wait until they're just about to kiss,
    Swaying in the heat in shift and sandal,
    Then magically turn Taylor Swift to Handel.

(The music changes to a Handel anthem. The fairies are unhappy about this and give **ROBIN** *a look, so he snaps his fingers and the music returns to rock and continues quietly in the background.)*

ROBIN. *(cont.)* Sometimes I go to visit Dairy Queen
    And worm my way into a Queen Machine
    Then turn myself into a soft ice cream.
    I wait till someone tastes me, then I turn
    To a chili pepper and I start to burn.
    I sizzle and I spark until they shout
    And have no recourse but to spit me out!
    One night to broomstick I attached a fork,
    Then snuck into a rooming house at dark.
    I tiptoed up the stairs, kept low for cover,
    And found on roof a hot tub made of rubber.
    Inflatable! Round and fat, the blow-up kind,
    For Guidos and Guidettes to soak behind.
    Indeed it made me think of Noah's Ark
    With porpoise next to porpoise, shark by shark.
    So sneaking up behind the tub, I pushed
    The fork and lo! the water wushed!
    They screamed and searched for clothes that they had
    worn,
    Now naked as the day that they were born!
    Hahaaaaa!

  (A rumble of thunder. **ROBIN** *looks up in alarm.)*

  But wait! Make room, fairy. Here comes Obcron!!

(Something extraordinary occurs in the atmosphere – a roll of thunder and a change in the sky – along with a wild electric guitar riff in the music – and **OBERON** *and* **TITANIA**, *the Fairy King and Queen, enter from opposite directions.)*

(They are extraordinary creatures – in looks, in dress, in attitude.)

OBERON. Ill met by moonlight, proud Titania.

TITANIA. What, are you jealous, Oberon?
    Fairies, skip hence! I have refused his bed and company.

(She starts to leave.)

OBERON. *Wait!* Am I not your lord and master?

TITANIA. Ha! Then I would be your lady, but I can't be that
because I know about your escapades and infidelities
with Harriet and Semele and Nausica and Ginger and–

OBERON. *THAT'S ENOUGH!*

(This is accompanied by a tremendous crack of thunder.)

How dare you, when everyone knows how you worship
that Governor Athens creature, and turned yourself
once into Hippolyta, his fiancée, to get a kiss and
cuddle from him, "Oh Chris dear let me handle your
constituents…"

TITANIA. These are the forgeries of jealousy;
And ever since the middle summer's spring,
Met we on hill, in dale, forest or mead,
By pavèd fountain or by rushy brook,
Or in the beachèd margent of the sea,
To dance our ringlets to the whistling wind,
But with your brawls, you have disturbed our sport!
The heavens open up,

(Crash!)

the rivers flood.
The tides go in and out at will so that
The fishermen are almost drowned by night!
The wind sucks up the fog and then it rains
For days and then it snows and rains again
and all this comes from our dissension
Which is caused by you!

ROBIN. Or it could be global warming, I suppose -

BOTH. *Shut up!*

*(**ROBIN** exits.)*

OBERON. The arguments of the gods have always changed
the weather here on Earth.

TITANIA. But we aren't gods, we're fairies.

OBERON. Technicality! And you *can* prevent all this, you know. You could stop it like *that! (snap!)* Just buy me the Mustang.

TITANIA. The horse?

OBERON. The *car*. And you know it.

TITANIA. Buy it yourself. You have the power.

OBERON. It's not the same thing! It's my birthday! I want a present! A present shows affection and without affection there's no relationship.

TITANIA. You should have thought of that before you fooled around.

OBERON. I didn't "fool around." I'm a fairy. It means I'm naturally gregarious!

TITANIA. Liar!

OBERON. Liar yourself!

(Slap! She slaps him hard across the face. He stares at her. Then slap! He slaps her back, just as hard. They glare at each other.)

OBERON. *(to the audience)* It's hard sustaining a relationship.

TITANIA. Fairies away!
We shall downright fight if I longer stay!

*(**TITANIA** takes up her train and sweeps out. **OBERON** is fuming.)*

OBERON. *(to himself)* Oh I will torment you for this injury. Puck! *Where are you?!*

ROBIN. *(appearing)* What's the prob?

OBERON. It's that *woman*. You'd think as a Fairy King I wouldn't have to put up with all this heartache. Now listen carefully. I have an idea. Do you remember how you and I once sat on that ledge over there overlooking this beach and saw Cupid, the God of Love, armed with his arrows? He took aim at one of the local girls and loosed his love shaft smartly from his bow -

ROBIN. I beg your pardon?

OBERON. He shot his arrow.

ROBIN. Oh.

OBERON. And he missed the girl, but the arrow landed on a little white flower that instantly turned purple. It was next to a discarded jar of hair pomade, that greasy stuff that all these hormonal teenagers use to streak their hair and make themselves think they're god's own gift to the opposite…what are you doing?

*(*ROBIN *is pomading his hair while checking himself out in a mirror.)*

ROBIN. Oh. Sorry.

OBERON. *Will you listen to me!!* Go fetch me that flower *now!* I assume you know its power.

ROBIN. Well…

OBERON. If you squeeze the juice of the flower on the eyelid of someone who's asleep, he or she will fall instantly in love with the first live creature that it sees.

ROBIN. Sounds big.

OBERON. You have no idea. Go fetch it immediately. I'll wait here.

ROBIN. "I'll put a girdle round about the earth in forty minutes!"

OBERON. Why?

ROBIN. To find the flower.

OBERON. But I just told you, it's right over there.

ROBIN. Oh. All right. I'll be right back.

(He exits.)

OBERON. *(alone, to the audience)* You see my plan, don't you. Once I have the juice, I'll put it on Titania's eyes when she's asleep. Then, when she awakes, she'll fall in love with whatever she sees first – be it a bear, or a monkey, or an ape! Ha ha! Though what *they* would be doing at the beach I have no idea. But who's that coming? I am invisible and I will overhear their conference.

*(*DENIS *enters, followed by* HELENE.*)*

DENIS. Helene, would you leave me alone! Now where are Lyle and Mia? You told me they were meetin' here to run away! ...You tricked me, didn't you?! Just to get me here!

HELENE. No, of course not!

DENIS. Then why are you following me?

HELENE. Because I can't help it! You're like a magnet to my heart. When you run away it's like I'm drawn to you.

DENIS. Have I said *anything* to lead you on? Haven't I been totally honest with you?

HELENE. Yeah. And I love you for that, too. I love you for everything. It's like I'm your dog, ya know. Your spaniel. You can whack me, you can ignore me, you can forget to feed me, it doesn't matter. I'll just drool on you and love you more.

DENIS. Look, just, just don't tempt me. All right? You could get yourself in trouble out here. You're a girl and it's dark out. And you're all alone except for me, and I could take advantage of you!

HELENE. It doesn't feel like night when I'm with you. It feels like day. And I'm not alone, cause you're the world to me, ya know?

DENIS. I'll run. I will, I swear, and leave you at the mercy of whatever comes along.

HELENE. It kinda doesn't matter. I'll just run after you anyway.

(She takes his hand and he pulls it away.)

DENIS. *Would you stop that!*

HELENE. *No!* And would you stop yelling at me! You hurt my feelings! *I'm the girl!* You're supposed to be chasing me! *You think I like this!!*

(He tries to answer her, but he's so frustrated and angry that he just grunts and gestures and jumps up and down and shakes his fist – and then he runs out.)

HELENE. *(to the audience)* He's just so cute when he gets mad like that.

I'm comin' after you!

And if chasing him turns all my life to hell,

I'll die upon that hand I love so well.

Whoa. Dramatic.

(She runs out after him.)

OBERON. Fare thee well, Nymph. Before you leave these woods, *he'll* be chasing after *you.* Ah, Puck.

ROBIN. I'm back.

OBERON. What are you doing?

ROBIN. Nothing.

OBERON. I mean what is *that.*

ROBIN. Where?

OBERON. Behind your back.

ROBIN. I don't see anything.

OBERON. You're holding something behind your back.

ROBIN. Oh I don't think so –

OBERON. *PUCK!*

ROBIN. *(bringing it out, almost swooning with excitement and pleasure)* Oh, sir, it is so magnificent. I won it last night at Bingo on the Beach! It's called an iPhone. You can do a thousand things with it. It's magic!

OBERON. We already do magic.

ROBIN. No, this is real magic. Watch this. Email. App Store. Angry Birds. *(or whatever's the hottest game app at the time of production)* Ohh! And here's the best part. Here, take this, I got you one. Now stand there.

(ring!)

Answer it, the green button.

(talking to the image in the phone)

"Hello, Oberon, can you see my face?" It's called Face-Time! Isn't it amazing!

OBERON. But I can see you there. In person.

ROBIN. Ah, but what if I were miles away?

OBERON. I'd call for you. You always come.

ROBIN. Well that's because we're fairies, but if we were mortal this would be indispensable.

OBERON. But we're not.

(He starts to toss it on the rocks.)

ROBIN. *NO!* Wait. It gives you... the weather.

OBERON. Sixty-eight degrees with a chance of rain.

ROBIN. Urban Spoon. You can find a restaurant.

OBERON. You do my cooking.

ROBIN. It has maps! Look! I can tell you the distance between Newark, New Jersey and Tuscaloosa!

OBERON. One thousand and eleven miles, so what's your point?

ROBIN. *It's not fair, you're immortal!!*

OBERON. All right, fine, it's very clever, very hip, now give me the flower.

ROBIN. Right. But. I was thinking. What if we transferred the magic from the flower to the iPhone. So instead of putting the juice of the *flower* in someone's eyes, we called them up. Beep bo! Beep bo! "Hello?" *Boing!* They're in love like *that!* A sort of post-modern flower. Wouldn't that be cool?

OBERON. Hand me the flower or I'll kill you.

ROBIN. Yes sir.

(He brings out the flower and it glows with magic. The flower is mysterious and very powerful.)

OBERON. I know a bank where the wild thyme blows,
Where oxslips and the nodding violet grows,
Quite overcanopied with luscious woodbine,
With sweet muskroses and with eglantine,
There sleeps Titania, sometime of the night,
Lulled in these flowers with dances and delight.

OBERON. *(cont.)* And there the snake throws her enameled
          skin,
          Weed wide enough to wrap a fairy in.
          And with the juice of this I'll streak her eyes.
          And make her full of hateful fantasies!
          Meanwhile, take thou some of it and seek
          Through this wood
          Until you find a sweet Italian girl who is
          In love with a muscle-head whose heart is flint –
          Anoint his eyes,
          But do it so the next thing he espies
          When he awakes may be the lady.
          You'll know him by his black pomaded hair,
          His Ray-Bans and his leather jacket.
          And do it carefully! so that he ends up
          Even more in love with her than she with him.
          Then meet me here before the dawn begins to glow.

ROBIN. You got it, Dude.

(a look from **OBERON***)*

                              I mean your servant shall do so.

*(***ROBIN*** gives him a thumbs up and leaves. ***OBERON***
shakes his head in despair. Suddenly there's a crash of
thunder, and the noise of it carries us straight into –)*

Scene Two

(Another part of the beach. Enter **TITANIA** *with her train of fairies. The thunderclap we heard was caused by Titania's anger.)*

TITANIA. That man makes me *so angry!*

MOONBEAM. Men do that. It's in their job description.

SUNFLOWER. The mortals even write songs about it. They call them country songs.

MOONBEAM. *(singing)* "She's my Honkeytonk Bedonkeydooooooonk!"

MUSTARDSEED. "Mah pickup truck's
Like mah rubber duck
But ah don't take it into the bathtub."

MOTE. "Kiss me honey
And kiss me twice,
Just don't give me dandruff
And don't give me lice."

COBWEB. "He was in the hospital
Covered in tubes,
Then he opened his eyes
And he stared at my – "

TITANIA. That's enough!

(gentle music)

Now come and sing to me a fairy song,
The kind that mothers croon when night is long,
And children in their heads are making toys
With drooping eyelids and remembered joys.
Then tell the beetles and the bats to go away,
And keep the canker worms and grubs at bay.
Then off to your duties
And let me rest.

(The fairies sing. The music is soft rock, something with the feeling of "Uptown Girl" by Billy Joel or "Can You

Feel The Love Tonight" by Elton John, about 20 seconds of it. It's quite beautiful and **TITANIA** *falls asleep.*)

MOONBEAM. Hence, away! Now all is well.

One aloof stand sentinel.

(*The Fairies exit. After a moment,* **OBERON** *enters and anoints* **TITANIA***'s eyelids with the nectar of the magic flower.*)

OBERON. What you see when you awake,

Do it for your true love take.

Love and languish for its sake.

Be it lynx or cat or bear,

Surfer dude with spiky hair,

Good old boy with gut of beer,

DJ with a cringing leer,

Wake when some vile thing is near!

(*He exits. As he exits,* **LYLE** *and* **MIA** *enter.*)

LYLE. We're lost! I can't believe it! I'm never lost!

MIA. You should have asked for directions! Oh! I am so tired! My back hurts, my bones are creaking. I feel like I'm thirty years old or somethin'.

LYLE Look, I'm sorry. I'll find the road in the morning, I promise. Let's bunk down here for tonight.

MIA. Oh all right. (*she sees a grassy spot:*) I'll sleep here.

LYLE. Ooh yeah, that looks comfy. We can share it.

(*He starts to lie down with her.*)

MIA. Uh, Lyle?

LYLE Yeah?

MIA. I think you should sleep over there.

LYLE. D'ya think? Wait. I feel some poetry comin' on.

Three blades of grass,

Two bodies,

One love.

(*He grins at her for approval.*)

It's called a Haiku. Which is a very short Swedish poem.

MIA. Hey, that's really good. And I got one for you, too. Let's see …

One love.

Two bodies.

And if you touch me before the wedding I'll kill you.

LYLE. Hey, c'mon! Nothin's gonna happen. I swear! Look, you've said to me that you love me as much as you love yourself. Right? So by lying here with me, you'll be alone, cause you'll be sleeping with yourself!

MIA. Now that's cute. *But,* if you slept here I'd feel like, oh what's the word, they use it in poetry all the time, it's a really fancy word, oh yeah, it's called a *SLUT!* So get your backside outa here and go over *there.*

LYLE. Okay, okay. *(he goes)* Feel better?

MIA. Yeah. Thanks. And just think, after we're married we'll be lyin' next to each other *forever.*

(He smiles…and then the implications of this hit him and he suddenly looks very worried.)

(MIA rolls over and falls asleep. Then LYLE shrugs and does the same. They both snore gently.)

(ROBIN enters)

ROBIN. Through the forest green and yellow

But I haven't spied the fellow.

He with greasy hair and shades

Who breaks the hearts of trusting maids.

Night and silence! There he is! Let's see… Ray Bans, leather jacket… That's the boy. And look at this. Separate beds. She probably wanted to sleep next to him but the churl said, "No! Sleep over there! I don't love you anymore!" I'll fix him good.

(He starts to squeeze the magic flower onto LYLE's eyes, but stops.)

ROBIN. Oh what the heck.

(He pulls out the iPhone and rubs it with the flower, thereby transferring the magic from the flower to the phone. Then he holds the phone to LYLE*'s ear.)*

ROBIN. *(cont.)* Into thy ear I send this power,
Formerly known as Purple Flower.

(He pushes a button: Beep bo! Beep bo!)

Sleep now but when you raise the sheet,
You'll fall in love with maiden sweet.
You'll beg her for her love and trust,
But she'll tell *you* to bite her dust.
Now don't awake until I'm gone,
For I must now to Oberon.
Hahahahahahaha!

(he runs off)

*(*LYLE *and* MIA *continue sleeping as* DENIS *runs in, chased by* HELENE. *They stop, both winded,* HELENE *especially.)*

HELENE. *(panting)* Stop! You're killin' me here!

DENIS. Good! Then stop followin' me!

HELENE. *(holding her side)* I gotta go to the gym more often…

(He starts to go.)

Wait! You wouldn't leave me here alone, would you?

DENIS. Why not? You started it. What do you want from me?!!

HELENE. Company?

DENIS. Well I don't want yours, so leave me alone!

(He runs off.)

HELENE. Denis! How could you do this to me!! *(to the audience)* It's just cause he thinks Mia's prettier than I am, but is that a reason? Everything nowadays is who's prettier, who's hot, who's juice. We live in a culture of celebrity and I hate that. Whatever happened to good old family values, like penmanship? I was good in school, you see, but that intimidated all the boys. So then I pretended to be stupid so they could feel macho. But it didn't work with Denis because he's always had this thing for Mia. The big schmuck. *(She takes out her compact to fix her makeup and sees herself in the mirror.)* Ahh! I look like a bear. No wonder Denis runs away. He thinks I'll hit him with my paw and throw him back in the stream. *(She looks in the mirror again.)* I hate mirrors. They never lie to you. *(Then, in the mirror, she sees* **LYLE** *lying on the ground behind her.)* Hey, there's Lyle. Hey Lyle! …Lyle…? *(shaking him, suddenly frightened that he might be hurt)* Lyle, please wake up and say you're fine!

*(***LYLE*** opens his eyes and we hear Ping! The sound of a bell. Whenever anyone falls in love instantly we hear the sound of a bell.)*

LYLE. I'll do more than that if you say you're mine.
Oh my God, I'm so in love with you!!

(She looks over her shoulder to see who he's talking to.)

HELENE. …Me?

LYLE. *(distraught with love)* You're like a goddess! You're like a flower in May!
Oh when I think of all the time we threw away,
And how we could have been together every day,
And I'd have kissed you till I had my way –

HELENE. *Okay, okay!* But what about Mia?

LYLE. Mia? Oh, please.
I liked her once but things like that just pass;
With her it's nag, nag, nag, what a pain in the

HELENE.   Ask
Me not to believe this!! You're making fun of me!?
Just cause Denis doesn't want me you're laughing at me?!
And I thought you were such a nice guy and you're hurting my feelings here!

LYLE. Helene, I would never hurt you!

HELENE. Get away from me! I'm gettin' out of here! G'bye!
And don't try to follow me cause I'm gonna cry!

(She races out.)

LYLE. Wow. She's a fast runner. I love that.
The truth is, I love everything *about* her.
How was it that I ever lived with*out* her?
Holy crap, so it must be love,
It's like I'm hit by lightning from above.
But there ya go, cause that's what women do.
They're soft and cute and make you feel like new.

(pumped)

Oh Love Gods, help me win Helene the brave!
And I will be her follower and slave!

(He runs off. Then **MIA** *wakes up.)*

MIA. Help! Lyle! Help me! I see a snake!
You've got to grab it off me! ...Hey, I'm awake!
I was sleeping. Oh my gosh. And now I'm waking.
Lyle, look at me and how I'm shaking.
There was this snake like pulling me apart.
He tore me limb from limb, and ate my heart
And Yuck! You just sat there and watched him while
I...Lyle? Where'd you go? Hey, Lyle?!
Lyyyyyle!! Yell back if you can hear me!!

(No answer. She hears frightening night sounds.)

I don't like this. I'm gettin' a little scared here.

(calls out) Okay, Lyle, I'm leaving!

And if I die, I'm tellin' everybody it was your fault!

(She runs off.)

(end of scene)

ACT THREE

Scene One

(Titania's bower. Enter the **CLOWNS**. *They don't see* **TITANIA** *asleep nearby.)*

PATTI. *(in high producer mode)* On time, all here, and it's the perfect setting for rehearsal. Now this flat part here will be our stage, we can change behind the shower.

NIKKI. Patti?

PATTI. Yes, oh Nikki Bottom?

NIKKI. I've been reading the script and I think there are parts that could be problems.

PATTI. Such as?

NIKKI. Well first of all, won't the audience be afraid of the lion?

PATTI. I've thought of that, so I've written a prologue. It's very post-modern. *(as if to us)* "Ladies and gentlemen. The part of the lion this evening will be played by Miss Janet Snug, Manicures. She's very sweet and doesn't bite people, except her mother when she gets excited." And then we'll fix the costume so that Janet's face can be seen coming through the lion's neck. Ergo no fear, problem solved.

OTHERS. Excellent. / Sounds good to me. *(etc.)*

ROBERT. Excuse me, but I see two more problems. First, the play says that Romeo and Juliet meet at night *under the stars.* But what if it's cloudy that night and we can't even see the stars?

PATTI. I've thought of that as well. We all have lights with us, now don't we. And we can *pretend* they're stars.

JANET. What do you mean?

49

PATTI. Our cellphones. They're always glowing. We'll just hold them up and let them drift across the sky like little stars and galaxies.

OTHERS. Ooh good idea. / Good thinking. / That's smart.

ROBERT. All right, but then there's the balcony. The play says, "Romeo and Juliet kiss on a balcony." And we don't have a balcony.

OTHERS. That's true. / He's right. (*etc.*)

NIKKI. …Wait. I'll solve this… Something's coming… Yes! I have it! One of us will *play the balcony*. She can lie on her back and hold her arms like *this* and we can put some railing at her fingertips.

ROBERT. I like it.

TERRI. That's perfect!

PATTI. Now let's start the rehearsal. You stand here. You here. And the rest of us are "offstage" at the moment in the "wings." Oh my god I love theater talk. Now Romeo, you begin, and when you've said your lines, you "exit" behind the trees and on we go from "cue to cue." Are we ready?!

*(Enter **ROBIN GOODFELLOW**.)*

ROBIN. What lusty locals have we lounging here
So near the cradle of the Fairy Queen?
It looks like Amateur Night at a church production
of *Our Town*.

PATTI. Speak, Romeo. Juliet, come forward.

NIKKI. "But soft, what kite through yonder window breaks?"

PATTI. "Light," not "kite!" "Light!"

NIKKI. Sorry. "What light through yonder window breaks?
It is the East, and Juliet is the sun.
Arise, fair sun, and kill the envious moon,
Who is already sick and pale with grease."

PATTI. *"Grief."*

NIKKI. You're sure it's not "grease?"

PATTI. *"Grief."*

NIKKI. Got it. And now I exit!

ROBIN. And I follow!

(*NIKKI exits, followed off by* **ROBIN**.)

FRANCI. Do I speak now?

PATTI. Yes, because you realize that Romeo has gone to look at a noise he's heard and he'll be right back.

FRANCI. "O Romeo, Romeo, wherefore art thou Romeo?
Deny thy father and refuse thy name,
Or, I'll no longer be a Catapult."

PATTI. "Capulet!" A *catapult* is a machine, dear. And Capulet is your family name, and Romeo's family name is Montague and they're all good Italian-Americans. Romeo! Stand by! She'll give you your cue again, and when you hear it, you should enter. All set?

NIKKI. (*off; muffled*) All set!

FRANCI. "Romeo! Romeo! Wherefore art thou, Romeo?!"

(*Enter* **NIKKI** *as Romeo, but transformed into an ass, i.e. wearing an ass head.* **ROBIN** *follows him on.*)

NIKKI. "O, speak again, bright angel, for thou art
As glorious as the neee-haaaaw!"

(*The girls and* **ROBERT** *see* **NIKKI**'s *transformation and they scream!*)

ALL. *Ahhhhhhhhhhhhhhhhhhhhhhhhh!*

PATTI. Ahh! How horrible! Girls, we're being haunted! Run, girls, run!

(*The girls run in circles and then run off.*)

ROBIN. (*chasing them*) *Hahahahahahaha!*

ROBERT. Oh, Nikki, what's happened to you?!

NIKKI. Where? Why? What? What are you talking about?! You're being an ass!

ROBERT. No, you are!

PATTI. Ahh! Oh bless you, Nikki. Bless you. You are translated!

(And the beauticians are gone.)

NIKKI. Oh, I get it. I see *exactly* what's going on here. It's a practical joke. They're trying to make an ass of me. But I'm not leaving no matter what they do. I'll walk around and sing so they can hear that I'm not afraid of them.

*(**NIKKI** sings the first four lines of a rock song with the feel of "I Want To Hold Your Hand" by the Beatles or "Honky Cat" by Elton John – something current to the production date of the play.* The last word of the song has a braying sound to it. **TITANIA** is awakened by the singing and sees **NIKKI**. Ping!)*

TITANIA. What angel wakes me from my flowery bed?

*(**NIKKI** sings another verse.)*

I pray you gentle mortal sing again.
Your voice is ravishing to my ear and I must
Confess, your shape brings out the girl in me.
What manner of man are you, good sir?
What knight of the realm with armor strong
Along with sword and buckler?
And in your face I see a virtue fair
That cannot help but make my heart declare
And swear I love you!

NIKKI. There's not much reason for that, now is there? I mean look at me, I need a shave. *Hee hawww!*

TITANIA. You are as wise as you are beautiful.

NIKKI. Well reason and love keep little company nowadays. If I was wise, I'd know how to get out of this place.

TITANIA. Out of this wood do not desire to go.
You must remain with me so we may know
The joys of love together. Hold me closer. *Closer.*

NIKKI. *(Groucho Marx)* If I held you any closer, I'd be behind you.

---

*See Music Use Note on page 3

TITANIA. I'll give you fairies to attend on you!
They'll pluck the wings from painted butterflies
To fan the moonbeams from your sleeping eyes.
I am a spirit of no common rate.
The summer still attends upon my state
And I do love you.
Peaseblossom! Cobweb! Mustardseed and Mote!

PEASEBLOSSOM. Ready!

COBWEB. And I!

MUSTARDSEED. And I!

MOTE. And I!

TITANIA. Be kind and courteous to this gentleman.
Hop in his walks and gambol in his eyes.
Feed him with apricocks and dewberries,
With purple grapes, green figs and honey.
Then bring him jewels and other treasures of the deep,
And shoo away the beetles so he'll sleep.

NIKKI. The Beatles? I love the Beatles! *"I wanna hold your haaaaaand!"*

TITANIA. Now Let It Be.

NIKKI. Oh, all right. We can still have A Hard Day's Night, can't we?

TITANIA. I'll take you on a Magical Mystery Tour.

NIKKI. Money Can't Buy Me Love, you know.

TITANIA. But I Saw You Standing There!

NIKKI. Where?

(She starts to caress him.)

TITANIA. All You Need Is Love.

NIKKI. Help.

TITANIA. I need somebody.

NIKKI. Help.

TITANIA. Not just anybody.

NIKKI. Help!

FAIRIES. *(singing)* YOU KNOW I NEED SOMEONE,
HELP!

(As **TITANIA** *leads* **NIKKI** *to her bower, the fairies continue to sing. They're joined by the soundtrack of the song they've chosen. Then just as* **TITANIA** *and* **NIKKI** *disappear into the bower, the lights change, the music intensifies and blares and the fairies launch into something very hip and very wild and fun to dance to – whatever is the hottest song at the time the show is produced. At the time of the first production, in late 2011, for example, it was the* LMFAO Party Rock Anthem ("Every day I'm Shufflin") *and the fairies – including the boy fairies of Oberon – danced up a storm. At the end of the excerpt, the stage snaps into black.)*

(intermission)

Scene Two

(Another Part of the Wood.)

(The act opens with an electric guitar riff, which is very loud, rude and wild, straight out of a rock concert. **OBERON** *is playing it, and he wears funky wire-rimmed sunglasses looking just as cool as all get out.)*

OBERON. I wonder if Titania is awake,
  And what it was that next came in her eye
  That now she dotes on in extremity.

  (Another riff. **ROBIN** *enters.)*

  How now, mad spirit. Spill the beans.

  (Chord!)

ROBIN. Where did you get it, sir? It's hot. *(i.e. the guitar)*

OBERON. I found it abandoned on the beach. *(short riff)* Is it not strange that sheep's guts should hale souls out of men's bodies?

ROBIN. Sheep's guts, sir?

OBERON. The strings of a guitar are made of sheep's guts.

ROBIN. Oh.

OBERON. And when they're plucked, the music creeps in at our ears and we are moved. Therefore the *guts* affect our *souls.*

ROBIN. Oh, that's good!

OBERON. You know I do say these rather profound things every now and then. You should listen. One day about four hundred years ago I was sitting right over there inventing quite a few of them – "To be or not to be" "Now is the winter of our discontent" – some really excellent gags, and this balding fellow with a quill pen scribbled them down and ran off. I wonder what happened to him? *(guitar riff!!)*
  Now tell me: Titania and the magic flower. What transpired?

OBERON. *(cont.)* Spin out the tale of her humiliation and
    disgracement,
    I long to hear what creature has explored in her abase-
    ment.

ROBIN. Well, sir…My mistress with a monster is in love.
    Ha!
    Near to her close and consecrated bower
    While she was in her dull and sleeping hour,
    Some local yokels were rehearsing a play
    Intended for the Governor's wedding day.
    The trick, you see, depended on one factor –
    To bide my time and separate an actor.
    So I waited till the star was out of view
    And as she stood there, anxious for her cue,
    I put an ass-head on her shoulders!

OBERON. Ha!

ROBIN. So then she hears her cue and out she streams,
    And like a startled bird her lover screams,
    And then the others running to and fro,
    Crying "Help!" and "Murder!" "Ye Gods!" and "Woe!"
    And one by one her fellows dissipated
    Until the last one cries "You are translated!"
    Hahahahahaha!

OBERON. But what about *Titania?*

ROBIN. Well isn't it obvious what then came to pass?
    Titania woke – and straightway *loved an ass!*

    (They both laugh.)

OBERON. Excellent! And did you then anoint the churl
    Who hurt the heart of wayward loving girl?

ROBIN. *(saluting)* Mission accomplished, sir!

    (Enter **MIA** *and* **DENIS.***)*

OBERON. Look, here he comes. The boaster with the tan.

ROBIN. Well that's the maiden but it's not the man.

MIA. What is the *matter* with you?! Have you got a screw
    loose?!

DENIS. Mia, please! I can take care of you! You don't need Lyle. Look. He abandoned you!

MIA. I don't believe that for one brazillionth of a second! Why would he do that, Denis? Lyle and I are a couple. We're runnin' away together.

DENIS. I don't know. Maybe you yelled at him or somethin'.

MIA. *I DON'T YELL AT PEOPLE!!* Hey. Wait a second. You *did* somethin' to him, didn't you? You-you-you *drugged* him or-or-or *distracted* him with some *cheap woman,* you son of a –

DENIS. Cheap woman? Where would I find a cheap woman around here?

MIA. *(shaking* **DENIS** *violently) Did you hit him?! Did you get violent with him?!*

DENIS. *Mia, stop!*

MIA. I'm findin' Lyle, you understand? *Now leave me alone!!*

(And she stomps off.)

DENIS. Talk about a high-maintenance woman, that girl is –

(SNAP! **OBERON** *has stepped forward and snapped his fingers, putting* **DENIS** *instantly to sleep.* **DENIS** *falls to the ground and snores as* **OBERON** *turns unhappily to* **ROBIN**.*)*

OBERON. You idiot.

ROBIN. But they look alike! I mean Ray Bans, leather jacket–

OBERON. Next time ask him his name first!
All right:
About this wood go swifter than caffeine
And find the girl from Jersey named Helene.
She'll be the tall one who looks sick and cries
Because she thinks her friend has prettier eyes.
By some illusion see you bring her here.
I'll charm this boaster's sight ere she appear.

ROBIN. I go, I go, look how I go,
Swifter than arrow from the Tartar's bow!

OBERON. Is this like that "girdle round the earth" thing?

ROBIN. Sort of. To show you how fast I am.

OBERON. How fast are you?

ROBIN. I can get her here in thirty seconds.

OBERON. Do it in ten.

ROBIN. Twenty.

OBERON. Twelve.

ROBIN. Fifteen.

OBERON. Done! It's a bet! Go!

> (**ROBIN** *takes off at a run.* **OBERON** *pulls out the magic flower and squeezes it into* **DENIS**' *eye, all the while reciting as fast as he can.*)

> Flower of this purple dye,
> Hit him like a cherry pie,
> Cupid's arrow mystify,
> When his love he doth espy.

> Let her shine like butterfly
> Or Venus of the starry sky,
> And when he wakes and she is by,
> She'll be the apple of his

ROBIN. Back!   **OBERON**. Eye!

OBERON. I can't believe it, it's a tie!

ROBIN. Captain of our fairy band,
> Helene the keen is here at hand!
> And the youth whose name is Lyle,
> Trailing her for mile and mile,
> Dodging from behind a tree,
> Pleading love on bended knee.
> Shall we their fond pageant see?
> Lord, what fools these mortals be!

> (**HELENE** *enters, trailed by* **LYLE**)

LYLE. Why would you even *think* that I'd make fun of you?! Look at me! Do I look like I'm havin' fun here? This is *love.* I'm *miserable!*

HELENE. But you're in love with *Mia!*

LYLE. Not anymore. Don't you listen to me?

HELENE. She's my best friend and we all grew up together– *(hitting him)* and I don't even like you anymore! I'm in love with Denis!

LYLE. *But Denis doesn't love you, you're not his thing.*

*(At which moment, **DENIS** wakes up and sees **HELENE**. Ping!)*

DENIS. Oh Helene, my love, would you accept this ring?
And swear to me that you are mine forever.
And promise me that you will never ever
Chase another guy.
My God, you make me want to cry!!
I love you!

HELENE. You are such a crud! Both of you! I can't believe this! So what are you, sitting around one day and you say, "I know, let's make fun of Helene today."

LYLE. Helene, I love you!

DENIS. Well I love her more! So go back to Mia.

LYLE. Hey, guess what? I'm givin' Mia up to you. She's yours. Congratulations.

DENIS. Oh no she's not. She's yours.

LYLE. She's yours!

DENIS. *But I don't want her!*

*(**MIA** enters and they both look at her.)*

MIA. Lyle, I've been lookin' all over for you! Why did you leave me?

LYLE. Why should I stay with you when love was calling to me.

MIA. "Love?"

LYLE. *(taking **HELENE**'s hand)* What else would you call it when you look into somebody's eyes and see the world?

MIA. What are you saying?

LYLE. I'm saying that I'm in love with *Helene.*

(beat)

MIA. …You must be sick. Come here, let me check.

LYLE. Would you cut it out. You are a pain in the neck!

HELENE. I don't believe this. *(to* **MIA***)* You're in on this, aren't you? It's not just them, it's all three of you! Mia! What happened to all the BFF, my best friend forever? We grew up together! We did our nails together! We went to concerts, ate ribs, played softball, texted, tweeted, we got dressed for dances together! You hypocrite! You double-dealing, two-timing, no good, lousy louse! *This isn't friendly and you're hurtin' my feelings!!*

MIA. I – I don't know what to say. Are you making fun of me?

HELENE. *Me?* You get Lyle to run after me and pretend that I'm the one he likes and then you get Denis here, the little weasel, to give me a *ring*, and I'm the one who's makin' fun of *you?!!*

MIA. I don't understand it …

HELENE. Okay, fine, keep it up. Make faces at each other when my back is turned. Here. Go ahead! …Ya finished? Cause I'm getting' outa here. *And if I die in this stinkin' woods tonight cause some pack of rabid chipmunks like attacks me when I'm not even lookin', let it be on all your HEADS!*

(She starts to stalk off.)

LYLE. She is so cute I could just…

MIA. Lyle? Are you makin' fun of her?

LYLE. Does *this* look like I'm makin' fun? *(He kisses* **HELENE.***)* Or *this*? Or *this*?

MIA. Lyle!

DENIS. *Just leave her alone! She's mine!*

LYLE. *She's mine!*

DENIS. *Do you wanna make somethin' of it?*

LYLE. *Yeah, I wanna make somethin' of it but I got a little problem here!*

(i.e. **MIA** *is hanging onto his leg)*

MIA. Am I a problem, Lyle? Is that what I am?! *(dancing like a boxer) Come on, take a swing! Let's go! I'll flatten you, you dumb ox!*

LYLE. *Hey!*

DENIS. *Watch it!*

LYLE. *Careful!*

HELENE. Is this how love can change us overnight
And turn what's right to wrong and wrong to right?

MIA. Oh shut up, Miss Know-It-All. You thief! You flirt! You *maypole!*

HELENE. Look who's talkin', the little puppet.

MIA. "Puppet?" *"PUPPET?"* Is that cause you're so tall and *wispy?* Cause you look like a *stick!* A *thread!* A piece of *dental floss with hair on top!*

(MIA *attacks* **HELENE,** *who ducks and weaves to get away from her)*

HELENE. Stop it! Get back! She may be short, but she's mean.

(MIA *screams and gets* **HELENE** *in a headlock.)*

Ow! Would you cut it out! I have *always* been there for you! Argh! I'll never follow you again, I promise!

(MIA *lets her go and* **HELENE** *gasps for air.)*

We've been friends ever since you were little. And believe me, you've been little for a long time.

MIA. Did you say little?

HELENE. Yeah, should I say short? Small? Tiny?

MIA. Lyle, did you hear that?!

LYLE. Oh be quiet, you dwarf.

MIA. What?

LYLE. Midget. Toe jam. Ear bud.

(with a cry, **MIA** *goes after* **LYLE** *now)*

DENIS. Helene, come on, we don't need this.

(He takes **HELENE** *by the hand and starts to lead her away.)*

LYLE. Leave her alone!

DENIS. So now you wanna make somethin' of it? Fine! Come on!

MIA. Denis, where are you going?

DENIS. I'm gonna kill him.

LYLE. Ha!

*(***LYLE** *and* **DENIS** *exit.)*

HELENE. *Denis, get back here!*

MIA. This is all your fault.

HELENE. My fault?! What are you, nuts?! Is your brain small, too, is that your problem?!

MIA. *Ahhhhhhhhhhhhh!*

HELENE. *Stop! Stop it! Heeeeeeelp!*

*(***MIA** *chases* **HELENE** *off.)*

*(***OBERON** *and* **ROBIN** *step forward.)*

OBERON. …You did this on purpose, didn't you?

ROBIN. No, King of Shadows, Great One, O Salam,
You said anoint the boy who had the tan.
And that's what I did!
But oh I've got to say it turned out right.
I mean, good Zeus above, did you see them fight!
Hahaaaaaaa!
Now it was him! Now it was her! Back and forth and *ding!* Round One is over! And there they go, back at it, he gives her a right to the chin, she dances back and delivers a left to the chest! He dodges, she parries and *ding!* Round Two! And now it's an uppercut straight to the jaw and he is *down for the count!* One, two, three, *and it's a touchdown!!*

OBERON. …Are you quite finished?

ROBIN. Yes. Sorry.

OBERON. You've messed up everything.

ROBIN. I know. That's what I do for a living.

OBERON. Fog.

ROBIN. Sorry?

OBERON. We need fog, and lots of it. Look:
> They just ran off to find a place to fight
> And therefore you must overcast the night
> So they can't see and never *find* each other.
> You can imitate their voices:
> "Lyle!" "Denis!"
> "Anyone for tennis?!"
> Then lead them up and down and wide and deep
> Until at last they're falling fast asleep.
> Then while they're snoring and in nightmare cry,
> You'll crush this *magic herb* in **LYLE**'s eye.

*(**OBERON** produces a vial with nectar in it.)*

ROBIN. What is it?

OBERON. It's the antidote. And do it this time!

ROBIN. Yes sir.

OBERON. *Lyle.*

ROBIN. Lyle.

OBERON. And not the other one.

ROBIN. Got it. I promise.

OBERON. While you restore the lovers to their ends,
> I'll to my queen and try to make amends.
> And then will I her charmèd eye release
> From monster's view, and all things shall be peace.

ROBIN. Solid.

*(**OBERON** shakes his head and exits.)*

ROBIN. Up and down, up and down,
> I will lead them up and down.
> I am feared in field and town.
> Goblin, lead them up and down.
> Here comes one!

(*Enter* **LYLE** *amid smoke and fog.*)

LYLE. Hey, Denis, where are you hiding, you coward!

ROBIN. (*as* **DENIS**) I'm right here, you creep! Where are you?!

LYLE. I'm comin' after you!

ROBIN. Follow me to the beach!

LYLE. Where?!

ROBIN. Once more unto the beach, dear friend, once more!

(**LYLE** *exits and* **DENIS** *stumbles in.*)

DENIS. Lyle! Lyle!

Tell me where'd ya go, are you in the hut?!

Or do you have your head crammed up your

ROBIN. (*as* **LYLE**)   But

You aren't here! So what are you wailing about?

You're the coward! You stand there and shout

"Hey, how ya doon! Hey look at me, the lover!"

But when I do show up you run for cover!

DENIS. That's it! I'm gonna kill ya!

(**DENIS** *exits and* **LYLE** *reenters.*)

LYLE. He was standing right here, I could hear his voice!

COWARD! WING-NUT!

Who needs all this? I'm tired and I'm sleepy.

To tell the truth, this whole thing's kinda creepy.

(*He sits down and yawns.*)

I've gotta sit and rest and won't despair,

Cause "sleep knits up the ravelled sleeve of care."

…I think that's from *Family Guy*. Zzzzz.

(*He falls asleep and snores. At which moment* **ROBIN** *enters leading* **DENIS** *with his voice.*)

ROBIN. (*as* **LYLE**) Hey, Denis! You scared to find me and tussle?

DENIS. Are you insane?! You're talkin' to "The Muscle!"
That's my nickname! And yours is "Little Wimp!"
Cause I'm the handsome one and you're the shrimp!

(sits)

Hey, what's goin' on? I feel so rotten.
It's like my brain is stuffed and full of cotton... Zzzzz.

(He drops over in sleep and snores. Then **HELENE** *enters.)*

HELENE. I started out with all my friends tonight,
But now I haven't got a friend in sight.
Mia was my pal there for a while.
And Denis was my life. And then came Lyle.
I want to just go home and go to bed!
But no, I think I'll try the ground instead
And sleep till daybreak comes and brings the light,
Cause things can change and wrongs can turn out right.
Zzzzzzzzzzzzzzzz.

(Enter **MIA**.*)*

MIA. Lyle owes me big-time for this mess.
I'm tellin' you, I never felt such stress!
I cannot tell you how this makes me mad.
Just look at me! I got scratches and my face looks bad.
I'd give my little finger for some liner,
Or Cover Girl to cover up this shiner.
I need some blush! Or lipstick for my mouth.
But now I think my legs are goin' south.
G'night, Ma. Zzzzzzzzzzzzzzz.

(She's out.)

ROBIN. Hahahahahaha!
Cupid is a knavish lad
Thus to make poor females mad.

*(**ROBIN** is about to use the phone on **LYLE**, but he sighs and throws it away. Instead he applies the nectar that **OBERON** gave him as the antidote.)*

ROBIN. *(cont.)* When thou wak'st, take true delight
In thy former lady's sight.
And the country proverb known,
That every man should take his own,
In your waking shall be shown.

Jack shall have Jill
Naught shall go ill.
The man shall have his mare again, and all shall be well.

(end of scene)

ACT FOUR

Scene One

(The beach. Rock music.)

(With the four lovers still asleep onstage, enter **TITANIA** *and* **NIKKI***, followed by Titania's fairies, then* **OBERON***, behind them all, unseen.* **NIKKI** *is still dressed as Romeo and still wearing the ass-head.* **TITANIA** *sits* **NIKKI** *down in a hairdresser's chair, which has been brought to her bower for the purpose. She's going to have the fairies "do"* **NIKKI***'s hair and nails – the ultimate joy for a hairdresser.)*

TITANIA. Come sit you down upon this flow'ry chair,
　　While with your mane of manliness I toy,
　　And style and decorate your coif of hair,
　　And kiss your darkling ears, my gentle joy.

　　*(**TITANIA** massages **NIKKI***'s hair.)*

NIKKI. Don't stop don't stop don't stop! Oooh. A little to the right.

TITANIA. How's that?

NIKKI. It's like I've died and gone to heaven.

TITANIA. I'll do it five more times.

NIKKI. No, make it seven.

　　Where's Mote and Mustardseed?

MOTE. I'm ready!

MUSTARDSEED. Here!

NIKKI. Now Mote, my dear, and Mustardseed, scratch my hooves a little, will you? Ooh, that's good, that's good. And now you can paint them with red for ravishing. Sunshine?

SUNSHINE. Yes, sir! Madam. Sir.

NIKKI. Sunshine, shine your rays of sunlight on those peaches there, they need some ripening. Then hand me a nice big glob of honey to go with it.

(sings first line of ABBA song:)

HONEY, HONEY, HOW YOU THRILL ME, UNH-HUH, HONEY-HONEY!

COBWEB. Are you peckish, Great One?

NIKKI. Peckish? I could eat a horse! *(looks down at herself)* Well not a horse perhaps, but something filling, like a bale of hay. Hay not only tastes good, but you can pick your teeth with it at the same time. And of course a peck of provender is nothing to be sneezed at.

TITANIA. I'll have one of my fairies fetch you

A bag of oats and nuts that has been hoarded

By a squirrel in winter.

NIKKI. I'd rather have a bowl of Quaker Oats, dear, I'm used to them. But wait…the very thought of food has made me sleepy. Let none of your fairies stir me now, for I simply must…get…my beauty sleep.

TITANIA. Rest, my darling.

And I will wind you in my arms, entwining

You as the ivy does the sturdy elm.

Oh how I love you! How I dote on you!

*(**NIKKI** and **TITANIA** sleep. **ROBIN GOODFELLOW** and **OBERON** enter. Or perhaps **OBERON** has been watching all of the above from a height.)*

OBERON. How now, young confusion. What thinkest thou?

ROBIN. I think confusion now has made his masterpiece. *(He bows.)* This would be quite a good time to buy that Mustang you've been wanting.

OBERON. That's not a "prob." I already have it.

ROBIN. You do? When, what, why, where, how?

OBERON. I met Titania in the woods and pointed out that she was doting on a donkey, my oh my. She said she couldn't help it, I said I know I made it happen. She

said the flower?, I said the flower and I'm the only one
who has the antidote. She said oh no, I said oh yes,
she said oh please, then came the tears and then the
screams, recriminations, accusations, after all it is a
marriage, so at last we came to an accommodation:
She wished me Happy Birthday from the heart
And said she loved me. And I love her.
And then she bought me the Mustang.
Eight cylinder, dual-cam, fuel-injected with bucket
seats.
I was touched.

(He holds up the keys.)

And now I will undo at last this hateful
Imperfection from her drowsy eyes.
You, my little beast of mischief, take the
Head from off this unsuspecting maid
That she and all the others scattered here
May join the Governor on his wedding day.
And please make sure
They think no more
Of this night's accidents
But as the fierce vexation
Of a dream.
But first I will release the Fairy Queen.

(He applies the antidote.)

Be as thou was meant to be.
See as thou was meant to see.
Antidote to Cupid's flower
Has this force and blessèd power.

*(**TITANIA** awakes.)*

TITANIA. Oh, my Oberon! What visions have I seen!

I thought I was enamored of an ass!

OBERON. There lies your love.

TITANIA. Ahhhhh! When, what, why, where, how?

ROBIN. That's what *I* said.

TITANIA. Oh, I don't like him at all any more.

(*Suddenly we hear a brass band playing "Hail to the Chief," approaching in the distance.*)

ROBIN. Fairy King, attend the mark.
I do hear the morning lark!

OBERON. Robin, quickly, off with her head.

(**ROBIN** *obliges.*)

Now, my queen, in silence pray,
We'll leave the night and join the day.
We'll trip around the globe and soon
We'll gaze upon another moon.

TITANIA. Come, my lord, and in our flight,
Tell me how it came this night
That I sleeping here was found
With these mortals on the ground.

(*The fairies disappear.* **GOVERNOR ATHENS** *and* **HIPPOLYTA** *hurry on in advance of their train of followers.*)

ATHENS. Hurry up!

HIPPOLYTA. Chris, we can't just disappear!

ATHENS. Of course we can. It's our wedding day. I love the beach. I love the music of the waves, the sounds that only we can hear and who the hell is that?

HIPPOLYTA. (*inspecting*) It's that boy and girl who wanted to get married.

(*At which point* **JUSTINE** *bustles in, dressed for the wedding. She's followed by a shy little man in a suit. His name is* **RUFUS** *and he tends to chew on the handle of his umbrella.* **JUSTINE** *and* **RUFUS** *are followed by* **PHYLLIS** *Trait and other members of the entourage.*)

JUSTINE. Oh, Governor, it's so exciting. But you shouldn't run off like that, we have a thousand things to do before the ceremony.

ATHENS. *(to* **RUFUS***)* Hello.

RUFUS. Hello.

JUSTINE. Oh, dear. I don't believe you've met my husband before. Governor Athens, Miss H, my husband Rufus.

HIPPOLYTA. How do you do.

RUFUS. Hello.

JUSTINE. He usually keeps to himself on public occasions. He's extremely shy.

RUFUS. Not really …

JUSTINE Rufus, don't contradict.

RUFUS. Yes, dear.

ATHENS. *(to* **RUFUS***)* I'm surprised we haven't met before.

JUSTINE. He's rarely seen, you see, because he usually has his dinner upstairs in his – *Ahh!* Mia? And there's Lyle and Denis and Helene. What are they doing here?!

ATHENS. Sleeping, I think.

JUSTINE. *Mia, wake up!*

MIA. *Ahh!*

HELENE. *What happened?!*

LYLE. How ya doon? How ya doon? Unh! Hey, what's goin' on?

HIPPOLYTA. *(amused)* That's what we want to know.

LYLE. *(groggy, not seeing* **JUSTINE***)* Well, let's see…I can't remember much except that Mia and I came here to get away from Mia's mother. Remember? She didn't even want us near each other. Ha. You know what we call her? We call her the Dragon Lady. *(He chuckles.)* Old Crab-Face. The Walking Pain in the aahhhhhhhh.

(He's facing **JUSTINE***.)*

JUSTINE. Old *what?!* Old *Crab-Face??!!*

LYLE. I-I-I wasn't talkin' about you! I was talkin' about the other Crab-Face…

JUSTINE. *That's enough!* We can all see *exactly* who you were talking about, and we know precisely what the Governor will do about it! Arrest that boy immediately!

ATHENS. What for?

JUSTINE. For abducting a minor!

(**RUFUS** *looks up.*)

And we caught them *just in time.* Denis, you must be so relieved.

DENIS. Well, to tell you the truth, I don't care what they do. I mean, all I know is, I'm in love with Helene.

(*He takes* **HELENE**'s *hand and she smiles happily.*)

(*This causes* **LYLE** *and* **MIA** *to embrace.*)

JUSTINE. Out of the question! (*to* **LYLE**) There is no way in the world you can marry a girl who's seventeen years old *so learn to live with it!*

(**RUFUS** *clears his throat.*)

RUFUS. Well …

JUSTINE. Rufus, be quiet.

RUFUS. I just wanted to say –

JUSTINE. Say nothing! I'll meet you back at the house.

MIA. Daddy, what is it?

RUFUS Well, you see your mother always wanted to keep you close to her for as long as possible, so she lied about your age when you were a little wisp of a thing. So you're really a few months older than she's been telling you.

MIA Two months? (*He shakes his head no.*) Four months?

RUFUS. No. Twelve months. You're eighteen years old.

(*Shock, then an explosion of joy and everyone cheers – except* **JUSTINE**.)

MIA. Oh, yes! Oh, Daddy! Oh, Lyle!

JUSTINE. Oh, hell.

HIPPOLYTA. It looks to me like a triple wedding.

ATHENS. (*to* **JUSTINE**, *shrugging innocently*) There's just no stopping impetuous youth.

The buds will blossom with leaves by the hour,

HIPPOLYTA. And nine months later, out pops the flower.

(She pats her stomach. She's expecting.)

ATHENS. What? Really?

HIPPOLYTA. Triplets.

(He staggers backward.)

ATHENS. Then sound the trumpets!

(The trumpets sound.)

And let's just hope I win reelection.

(The offstage band plays "Hail to the Chief" as everyone but the four lovers leave the stage. The lovers watch them go, then look at each other, unsure what to think.)

MIA. …Do you remember anything from last night after we got here?

DENIS. Not really.

HELENE. I can almost remember.

LYLE. These things seem far away and small, like mountains turning into clouds.

DENIS. Whoa. That's like profound.

LYLE. It's from a play by Shakespeare.

HELENE. Which one?

LYLE. William.

(The couples walk off, hand in hand. When they're gone, NIKKI awakes and rises from Titania's bower.)

NIKKI. Hey! Wake me up for my cue, okay, and then I'll answer it. I think it's "Romeo, Romeo! Wherefore art thou, Ro – …" …Hello?! Patti?! Franci?! Roberta?! They left me here asleep? I can't believe it. And yet… I have had a most rare vision. I have had a dream past the wit of woman to say what dream it was. A girl would be an ass to try and explain this dream. I thought I was – …I thought I saw – …I thought I *had* – …Don't go there, lady, we're confused enough. …No woman's eye has heard, no woman's ear has seen, no hand has tasted, no tongue conceived and no heart can report what my dream was. I'll get Patti to write a song about it. We'll call it "Nikki Bottom's Dream" because it has no bottom, and I'll sing it at the end of the play in front of the Governor. The Governor…? Oh my gosh, the play! I almost forgot! *Patti, don't start without me!*

(She runs off. End of scene.)

Scene Two

(enter the hairdressers, distressed)

PATTI. Have you checked at Nikki's house?! Is she home yet?

ROBERT. No, she isn't home. She was transported.

JANET. Poor Nikki.

FRANCI. If she doesn't come back, I suppose the play is out.

PATTI. Of course it's out! There isn't a beautician in New Jersey who could play Romeo the way she does.

JANET. She has more talent in her little finger than any other hairdresser in the state!

*(**TERRI** runs in.)*

TERRI. Girls, the Governor and his wife are coming back from the ceremony, and two other couples were married at the same time! If our play gets chosen we'll be famous!

FRANCI. Oh, Nikki! Please! Where are you when we need you?!

*(The girls look heavenward. They clasp their hands in prayer, close their eyes and start moving their lips, praying silently. **NIKKI** enters behind them. She sees what they're doing…gets in line, clasps her hands and starts praying with them. Then she whispers to **FRANCI**:)*

NIKKI. What are we doing?

FRANCI. *AHHH!*

ALL. Nikki! / Oh, Nikki! / Most courageous day! / Most happy hour! / She's back!

NIKKI. Girls, the most wonderful things have happened! But don't ask me now, we have work to do!

ROBERT. Work?

TERRI. What do you mean?

JANET. Nikki!

NIKKI. The Governors have narrowed it down to three possible entertainments, and *we are one of them!*

("Hurray!" / "Oh my heart!" / "Oh, Nikki!")

We are to go immediately to the mansion and wait. Now I want you to look over your parts *with your eyes closed and no peeking!* It must be in your head and not on the page. And don't forget to check your breath, if you had onions for lunch you have to brush or we're done for. And finally, girls, remember that at the end of the day we may not get chosen by the Governor, but we have to keep our heads high and *"O for a muse of fire that would ascend the brightest heaven of invention!"* So please, for heaven's sake *DON'T GET EXCITED!* We have a motto and we must stand by it!

ALL. Scissors up
Nails bright
Combs down
Curlers tight.

Dryers on
Extra fluff
Hit the spray
And that's the stuff!

(They cheer and exit.)

ACT FIVE

(The lawn of Governor Athens' mansion. The four lovers run in, elated and boisterous. They've just come from the triple wedding and they're dressed to the nines. **GOVERNOR ATHENS** *and* **HIPPOLYTA** *follow them on; then* **PHYLLIS, JUSTINE, RUFUS,** *and attendants.)*

LOVERS. *Whoooo! / Whooo! / Married! / We're married!! / Holy cow!*

HELENE. *(flashing her wedding ring)* Hey, Gov, did ya see this?!

ATHENS. Fantastic.

HIPPOLYTA. It's gorgeous!

HELENE. Not too bad for a girl who works at the Lobster-Knobster, huh?

LYLE. How ya doon, how ya doon?

DENIS. Hey, Rufus. I guess you been down this road before, huh?

RUFUS. Yes, yes I have. And good luck to you. *(taking* **HELENE***'s arm rather amorously)* Hello, my dear. You're looking lovely this evening …

ATHENS. Phyllis, the play you arranged - do we have a winner?

PHYLLIS. I have it down to three choices. Would you like to read about them?

HIPPOLYTA. Let's see. "The Three Sisters: a brief adaptation of Chekhov's masterpiece, with Russian dressing, enacted in mime with hand-puppets."

ATHENS. I was in that play in college and by intermission even the audience threatened to leave for Moscow.

HIPPOLYTA. Let's see what else… "Yee-Haw: a country musical with a rodeo and a steer. Barbecue to follow."

ATHENS. It sounds gruesome and athletic at the same time.

HIPPOLYTA. "Romeo and Juliet: a tediously brief and rollicking tragedy of suicide, destruction, and Scottish dancing, presented by the staff of Hair and Gone, the finest Beauticians East of the Atlantic."

ATHENS. Tedious yet brief? Rollicking yet tragic? Is that possible?

PHYLLIS. Yes sir, it is. I've read it. It's short, but it feels endless. And they've kept the tragedy but tried to improve it.

HIPPOLYTA. Improve *Romeo and Juliet?*

PHYLLIS. They've changed the dialogue and added a lion.

HIPPOLYTA. Does he talk?

PHYLLIS. I'm afraid so, ma'am.

ATHENS. How's the death scene?

PHYLLIS. Hilarious, sir. After the first two characters die, you just keep wishing the rest of the cast would take the hint.

HIPPOLYTA. And who are these beauticians that play it?

PHYLLIS. They're simple people, ma'am. They say they've never acted before, but apparently that's an understatement. They've decided that the one who remembers the most lines gets a prize.

HIPPOLYTA. I like them already. Tell them they're on.

ATHENS. Agreed.

PHYLLIS Oh, no ma'am. Please. You mustn't. I heard them rehearsing and it was embarrassing.

ATHENS. Have you ever *studied* Shakespeare, Phyllis?

PHYLLIS. No sir.

ATHENS. He has one of his heroes say that
   "never anything can be amiss
   When simpleness and duty tender it."
   Shall we be Shakespeareans, Phyllis?

PHYLLIS. If you say so, sir.

ATHENS. Good, go call them. Ladies and Gentlemen, take your places.

(As they take their seats for the entertainment, we over-
hear **HELENE** *and* **DENIS** *talking:)*

DENIS. Hey, you can't leave the Lobster-Knobster. You're a
waitress. You make good tips.

HELENE. Yeah, but I want to go back to school and learn
how stuff works, ya know?

DENIS. *(patronizing)* You mean like cars and stuff, right?
You don't have to worry, I got it covered.

HELENE. I mean like business stuff. We'll have to support
ourselves. Take Lobster-Knobster. It's a franchise,
right?, with each branch capitalized around a mil-
lion-six-five-oh, including site repair and fixtures. So
I figure I could buy one if I leveraged the cost at an
even 5% with the current discount rate, then invested
the excess on margin in some techno-stocks I've got
my eye on.

DENIS. ...Yeah, that's good. Go back to school.

(Enter the **PROLOGUE** *onto a makeshift stage. It's*
JANET. *She's terrified at being the center of attention.)*

JANET. *(as* **PROLOGUE**)
"Good sirs. And madams.
If we offend you, it's because we've tried.

To not offend you, but to give you pleasure.
We pray that you enjoy our play, especially
At the end when we expose ourselves.

To the wonders of the human spirit,
Which are so tremendous that mere words
And gestures can convey it."

PATTI. "Can *not* convey it."

JANET. "*Not* convey it." Do I have to say all this? I just want
to tell them to enjoy themselves.

PATTI. Just say your part!

JANET. "The actors are at hand to tell us true
That life is more than haircuts and shampoo.
That life is love and death and all between,

JANET. *(cont.)* Which in our humble play will now be seen."
We hope you like it.

(**JANET** *rushes the last two lines, then bows and rushes off the stage. The lovers clap.*)

MIA. I thought it was good how she memorized it.

LYLE. I had to memorize a poem in high school once about Paul Revere. I must have been good cause I remember the teacher crying and shaking her head.

HELENE. Shhh. Here they come.

(*Enter* **PATTI** *as* **CHORUS**, **NIKKI** *as* **ROMEO**, **FRANCI** *as* **JULIET**, **ROBERT** *as the* **BALCONY** *and* **TERRI** *as the moon.* **ROBERT** *holds two balusters and anything else that makes him look balcony-like; and* **TERRI** *holds a lantern, a branch and a dog.*)

PATTI. *(as* **CHORUS**, *introducing the actors)*
"Dear friends, you may be wondering why we're here,
So wonder on till truth makes all things clear.
This lady fair is Juliet, she of woe,
This handsome man is none but Romeo.
This woman* is the balcony that holds
Aloft the lovers with her plaster molds.
Scene one involves all three of these plus Moon,
Whose presence lights the scene and makes night noon.
And last of all we introduce the Lion,
Frightful, ferocious, fearful Hound of Zion.

(**PATTI** *motions to* **JANET** *to come on stage. She does, reluctantly, wearing a lion costume from which her head protrudes.*)

With jaws of iron and with dripping snout,
The beast that Shakespeare inadvertently left out.

TERRI. Our play begins when lo! by lucky chance
Our lovers fall in love at ancient dance.

---

* Change "woman" to "fellow" if the character is Robert as opposed to Roberta.

JANET. Then Romeo goes to garden feeling jealous,
    Sees Juliet above and climbs her trellis.

FRANCI. Then later in a setting all but merry,
    The lovers meet at night in cemetery.

ROBERT. There does Romeo find his lover slain,
    With torso washed in lion's crimson stain.

NIKKI. Whereat with blade, with bloody blameful blade,
    He bravely broached his boiling bloody breast,

FRANCI. Then Juliet, returning from night's shade,
    Her dagger drew and died and came to rest.

DENIS. These guys are good! I feel like moved already.

HELENE. Shh. The balcony is about to speak.

BALCONY/ROBERT. "In this same interlude by light of torch,
    Tis I, Robert, who will play the porch.
    A porch whose railing Juliet is clutching,
    Keeping Romeo and Juliet from touching.
    Alas, I think the story would be gladder
    If only Romeo had brought a ladder."

HIPPOLYTA. And here comes Romeo!

ROMEO/NIKKI. "O grim-looked night! O night with hue so black!
    O night! O night! Alack, alack, alack!
    And thou, O balcony, which soon will hold
    My lover's feet or else will quickly fold.
    And then she'd fall
    And hit the wall,
    Or bounce like ball.
    And oh, if only I could *see her now*!"

(NIKKI glares at TERRI, who is holding the lantern aloft – but TERRI has forgotten to turn it on. TERRI gasps and turns it on with a click.)

    "But soft, what light breaks yonder window least?!
    It is my love who rises in the East,

ROMEO/NIKKI. *(cont.)* Who makes her lover Romeo rise as
well,

And kill the envious moon as heart doth swell."

JULIET/FRANCI. *(entering onto balcony)*
"O Romeo, Romeo, wherefore art thou Romeo?

Deny thy father and refuse thy name,

Or I'll no longer be a Catapult."

PATTI. Capulet! Capulet!

JULIET/FRANCI. Well I'm sorry, they sound the same!
"Tis but thy name that is my enemy."

(That's an understatement.)

"Thou art thyself, though not a Mongoose."

PATTI. "Montague!"

JULIET/FRANCI. *"What's in a name?!…That which we call a rose
By any other word would smell as sweet!"*

ROMEO/NIKKI. "I see a voice! O now up wall I climb
To join my love and challenge ticking time."

(He climbs up onto the balcony.)

ROBERT. Ow!

ROMEO/NIKKI. Sorry.
"O love, at last your visage in I drink!"

JULIET/FRANCI. "My love! Thou art my Romeo I think."

ROMEO/NIKKI. "And I, like Paris, shall be always true."

JULIET/FRANCI. "As Angelina is to Brad, so I to you."

ROMEO/NIKKI. "Let me kiss you in your bedroom and your
hall."

JULIET/FRANCI. "You may kiss me on my balcony, that's all."

ROMEO/NIKKI. "Then marry me, I beg, at break of day!"

JULIET/FRANCI. "Tide life, tide death, I come without
delay!"

(They exit.)

BALCONY/ROBERT. "Thus have I my part dischargèd so,
And being done, so Balcony does go."

(She/he bows and exits)

MIA. Look, here comes a priest.

FRIAR/TERRI. "No, I the *Friar* am and be it so
  I married Juliet to Romeo.
  I did it 'gainst their parents' grave advice,
  And now I do regret this roll of dice.
  For Romeo was banished on the morrow,
  And Juliet was filled with grief and sorrow.
  Then I, the Friar, had a tragic notion
  That grieving Juliet should take a potion.
  It seemed a good idea in many ways;
  Alas, the potion made her sleep for days.
  And now sleeps Juliet in peaceful coma,
  While nearby beast smells succulent aroma."

LION/JANET. "Roar."

HELENE. Look! The lion speaks!

LION/JANET. "You ladies, you whose gentle hearts do shrink
  At smallest mouse you find on floor or sink,
  Should know that I am Janet, who does nails,
  And not a lion real with claws and tails.
  For if I entered now as lion true,
  You'd probably get scared and call the zoo."
  This is where I attack Juliet.
  I'm sorry.

(Lion "attacks" the sleeping Juliet).

  "Roar. Growl. Devour."

(Juliet raises a blood-red handkerchief and waves it.)

JULIET/FRANCI. "Ah!"

MIA. Did Lion just kill Juliet?!

FRANCI. No ma'am. But he has drawn blood, which Romeo
  will see and mistake for death. We all fear death and
  see it everywhere.

MIA. And here comes Romeo!

ROMEO/NIKKI. "Sweet Moon, I thank thee for thy beams so bright, for now I'll see my Juliet in the light.

(He looks around, then down and sees JULIET sprawled at his feet.)

But stay! O spite!

But mark, poor knight,

What dreadful dole is here!

Eyes, do you see!

How can it be!

O dainty duck! O dear!

Come, tears, confound!

Out, sword, and wound

The pap of Romeo;

Ay, that left pap,

Where heart doth hap.

Thus die I, thus I go.

Now am I dead

Now am I fled;

My soul is in the sky.

Tongue, lose thy light!

Moon, take thy flight!

Now die, die, die, die, die."

LYLE. … I think he's dead.

MIA. *(apprehensive)* Yeah, but it's just play-acting, right? He's not really hurt, is he?

DENIS. We'll find out soon. Juliet's getting up.

MIA. But wait. The Moon is gone and she has no lantern. How will Juliet even *see* Romeo?

HELENE. Hold it. Look!

(The cast members have taken out their cell phones and turned them to "bright." They wave them slowly across the sky, humming in imitation of the music of the spheres.)

It's the stars! She'll see by starlight!

PATTI. That's right, my dear. It's meant to create atmosphere for the final scene, which is very tragic but also inspiring. Go ahead, Franci.

JULIET/FRANCI. "Asleep, my love?

What, dead, my dove?

O Romeo arise!

Speak, speak. Quite dumb?

Dead? Dead? A tomb

Must cover thy sweet eyes.

These lily lips,

This cherry nose,

These yellow cowslip cheeks

Are gone, are gone!

Lovers make moan;

His eyes were green as leeks.

Tongue, not a word!

Come, trusty sword,

Come, blade, my breast imbrue!

(She stabs herself.)

And farewell, friends.

Thus Juliet ends.

Adieu, adieu, adieu."

(Silence. The onlookers are strangely affected. Then they clap and the cast bows.)

CAST. Thank you./Thank you!

NIKKI. Would you like to hear the Epilogue? It's very moving.

ATHENS. No Epilogue is needed, for the play needs no excuse. If you could do some humming and dancing, however, it would help us greatly.

PATTI. Girls?

(The girls begin humming something inspiring, along the lines of You've Got A Friend, *or Katy Perry's* Fireworks. *There should be a gentle orchestration behind*

*it, as everyone dances behind the actors who speak the
final words of the play. The dancers still have their cell
phones out, so the sky is alight with seemingly hundreds
of stars twirling and dipping.)*

ATHENS. *(over the music)* The iron tongue of midnight has
told twelve.

Lovers, to bed. It's almost fairy time.

*(**ATHENS** and **HIPPOLYTA** take hands and join the
dancers.)*

LYLE. So whatdya say? D'ya think we'll be happy together?

MIA. Are you kiddin'? We'll be such a great couple we
could be on television.

(They join the dancers at the back.)

HELENE. I always knew I'd get you in the end, ya know. It
was just a matter of time.

DENIS. Yeah, me too. I was playin' hard to get, that's all.

HELENE. Oh you are so full of it. C'mere.

*(She kisses **DENIS** beautifully and they join the dancers.)*

(All is magic now.)

*(Enter **OBERON**, **TITANIA**, **ROBIN** and all the rest of the
FAIRIES. The **FAIRIES** join the dancers.)*

OBERON. Now until the break of day,
Through this house each fairy stray.

TITANIA. So shall all the couples three
Ever true in loving be.

BOTH. Trip away. Make no stay.
Meet us all by break of day.

*(**ROBIN** steps forward as the song continues in the background.)*

ROBIN. If we shadows have offended,
Think but this, and all is mended,
That you have but slumbered here
While these visions did appear.

And this weak and idle theme,
No more yielding but a dream,
Gentles, do not reprehend:
If you pardon, we will mend:
Else the Puck a liar call;
So, good night unto you all.

Pow!

(Music. Dancing. Or just a shaft of light illuminating **ROBIN**, *fist raised with enthusiasm – and the stage goes black. The important thing is to end on a note of triumph and joy.)*

End of Play